Elizabeth Champney

In the Sky Garden

Elizabeth Champney

In the Sky Garden

ISBN/EAN: 9783337036300

Printed in Europe, USA, Canada, Australia, Japan

Cover: Foto ©Andreas Hilbeck / pixelio.de

More available books at **www.hansebooks.com**

BY

LIZZIE W. CHAMPNEY.

ILLUSTRATED BY J. WELLS CHAMPNEY.

("CHAMP.")

BOSTON:

LOCKWOOD, BROOKS, AND COMPANY.

1877.

TO

PROFESSOR MARIA MITCHELL,

THIS LITTLE BOOK OF FABLES OF ASTRONOMY,

WRITTEN IN THE HOPE OF INTERESTING THE SMALL PEOPLE,
AND LEADING THEM TO A STUDY OF ITS
MORE FASCINATING TRUTHS,

Is Gratefully and Lovingly Dedicated

BY HER PUPIL AND SATELLITE,

THE AUTHOR.

TABLE OF CONTENTS.

TABLE OF CONTENTS.

PEEP THE LAST.

THE TAIL OF A COMET.

"Oh, stars wreathed vinewise round yon heavenly dells,
  Or thrust from out the sky in curving sprays,
Or whorled, or looped with pendent flower-bells,
  Or bramble-tangled in a brilliant maze,
Or lying like young lilies in a lake
  About the great white Lily of the moon,
Or drifting white from where in heaven shake
  Star-portraitures of apple-trees in June,
Or lapped as leaves of a great rose of stars,
  Or shyly clambering up cloud-lattices,
Or trampled pale in the red path of Mars,
  Or trim-set quaint in gardeners' fantasies!"

SIDNEY LANIER.

PEEP THE FIRST.

TRAINING THE POLE-STAR.

THE SPIRIT OF RAIN

"DIDN'T know that stars needed trellises," said Joy.

"They don't generally," replied Puck; "but, you see, this is the pole-star, and I have to tie it to the pole every night: if I didn't, it might droop down or wabble about, and then what would be the good of the nautical almanac?"

"How dreadful it would be, if you should forget!"

"But I never do, you see. I play when I play, and work when I work. I cut up all manner of capers down in your foolish world; but up here in the sky-garden I attend to business. My work is done now, however; and, if you like, we will take a stroll."

This was all a dream, of course, — a queer dream that Joy Fairchild had, once upon a time. She had rambled about all night in the beautiful sky-garden overhead; but what she had seen had been so little in comparison with its whole extent that it was really nothing but a peep, after all.

It was not so very unlike one of our earthly gardens. Angel-children were watering and tending the star-flowers, which were not all white or colorless, as seen from the earth, but quivered and flamed with gorgeous hues like the flashing gem-fruits that grew in the grotto, in the story of "Aladdin and the Wonderful Lamp." She saw them hang above her in the trees, —

> " And twinkle and burn and glow
> Like brilliant rhombs of Iceland spar
> When pierced by the sun's bright bow.
> And some were grouped in mystic curves,
> And angles and spheres and zones
> And prisms that on their axes burn,
> As well as glittering cones."

She walked, too, upon a mosaic of them, that in shape and color resembled the patterns in her kaleidoscope at home.

There were white ones too, — tiny silver spangles,

14

they seemed; but these were the snow-crystals, with leaves and stems of cut or spun glass, that grow fastest on the coldest winter nights. Joy did not mistake them for stars, though they were similar in shape, and some parts of the sky-garden were filled with them.

She was not surprised to see that the star-flowers were not all white; for Joy's father was an astronomer, and had told her of the exquisite colors which some of them display in the telescope: how the double stars, especially, loved to show brilliant complementary colors, taking just the hue that would contrast most charmingly with that of the star that blossomed nearest, — a rose-colored star beside an emerald one, a deep sapphire-blue with a pale yellow primrose for a neighbor, white and ruby, gold and purple, sea-green and orange, — each enhancing the beauty of the others. She had never been able to make out these colors for herself before; but now that she found herself close to them, the tints were very vivid and distinct.

The strangest thing of all to Joy was, that every thing here should seem so perfectly familiar, being exactly what she had expected. It was not a lonely garden, by any means. She saw people moving about with whom she had long been acquainted in fairy-tales. Dear North Wind swept by, with "Little Diamond" clinging in her hair. Joy wanted to creep up behind too; but they passed like a flash, and did not notice her. The wonderful trunk that kind-hearted Hans Andersen left behind him sailed along more leisurely; and Joy could see that it was filled with merry children: indeed, it was so full that there was no room for her. There were plenty of people from "Mother Goose;" but Joy had outgrown their society, and could not remember having ever cared very much for them, they were such a crazy, nonsensical lot.

A mischievous-looking little boy was training a tall and slender star-stalk to a staff. Joy watched him at his work. He did not seem too busy to notice her, for he nodded good-naturedly as she approached, and answered all her questions as politely as though he were placed there on purpose to grant information to little pilgrims from the earth. His name, he told her, was Puck; and Joy gratefully accepted the invitation to walk with him in this wonderful garden.

"That is Rainbow Bridge, that the spirit is standing on," said Puck; "and just beneath is Cloudland. Some day perhaps we will go there together. It is an interesting country, full of ghosts and goblins, but not nearly so beautiful as our garden. Do you like bugs?"

The question was so abrupt that it startled Joy, and she replied dubiously, "Some kinds."

"Well, come this way with me: I want to show you some curious insects that feed on our flowers."

What queer things they were, buzzing about like

beetles or dragon-flies from flower to flower! When Joy examined them attentively, she saw strange tubular antennæ protruding from their heads, which they were continually whisking about in the most eccentric way, pointing them at the star-flowers, shortening and extending them, but never quite touching the blossoms. This made her think that these queer appendages were not, as she had at first fancied, trunks and tubes through which they sucked honey, but eyes of similar organism to those possessed by certain beetles that she had heard Uncle Briar talk about,— insects that could contract or lengthen them like the tubes of an opera-glass, swelling or flattening the lenses so as to make magnifying-glasses of different powers ; just as there are others that concentrate upon the same point a great number of microscopic eyes.

When Joy mentioned this to Puck, he smiled good-naturedly. "You are not so stupid as you look," he remarked, by way of encouragement. "These funny bugs, as you call them, are scientific men, whose eyes have become so accustomed to their work that they shoot out telescopes and microscopes of their own, and come up here in their dreams to carry on their observations. That very solemn beetle, watching the comet, is your father. Some of the most remarkable astronomical discoveries have been made in this way. You see they get a great deal nearer to the stars here; and, by looking intently, what they see becomes photographed upon their eyes, so that when they next look into a telescope during their waking hours they see it again; and as they have forgotten all about their dream, they fancy they see it for the first time. There is only one trouble about it. Sometimes, when they have been observing snow-flakes with their microscopic eyes in their sleep, they will, when awake, next look at some heavenly body, and then they are liable to make some astonishing assertion like this: that 'It is all a vulgar mistake to suppose that Saturn is now surrounded by concentric rings, for when last attentively observed by me they had disappeared, and the planet had assumed the shape of a hexagonal crystal, with connecting alabaster spars, much resembling one of my wife's patterns for crocheting a tidy.' Or perhaps it will be a microscopist, who has been using his telescopic eyes at night; and he writes, in the report which he is to read before the State Medical Convention, that he believes he is 'the first to make the very important discovery that the sporadic germs of certain contagious diseases are lighted by seven suns, of which the principal one is indigo blue, the secondary orange, three minor ones white, and two exceedingly minute ones like little ruby eyes.' And this, you know, sounds like nonsense to some people."

Joy was a little tired of Puck's talk about the scientific beetles. It seemed to her that he was making fun of her; and she was on the point of resenting his assertion, that one of those strange insects could be her father, when her attention was attracted by some beautiful cobwebs suspended from some of the star-trees. They were gemmed with dewdrops, and resembled the very finest lace-work; they were so beautiful that Joy could not help wishing that the old woman in " Mother Goose," whose business it was " to sweep the cobwebs out of the sky," would not find them.

Puck saw her admiring them. " Your father would call those gauzy things ' nebulæ,' " he said. " How would you like one of them for a lace shawl ? "

Then Joy remembered all that her father had ever said about the nebulæ, — how the resolution of these fancifully shaped hazy clouds into clusters of stars was

one of the most interesting problems of the day. He
had showed her a space in the heavens filled with this
irresolvable star-dust and stars mixed. The nebula
formed an irregular lace whose pattern was marked out
by the stars; and she had spoken then of the beautiful
bridal veil it would make. Then her father had showed
her pictures of the fantastic forms of many of Lord
Ross's and of Herschel's nebulæ; the dumb-bell, the crab,
the horse-shoe, the grotesque face in Ursa Major, and
the nebula in Berenice's hair which only needed the
addition of a comb or a few hair-pins to bear a marked
resemblance to a switch. Joy wondered what could
have been the unlucky accident that hung it in the sky-
garden, so far from the head of the hapless Berenice.
Perhaps she was playing croquet the night of the great
meteoric shower, and lost it in her excited chase after
the fiery balls. . She had heard, too, of the beautiful
nebula in the Southern Cross, composed of one hundred
and ten stars, of which eight of the more conspicuous
ones being colored various shades of red, green, and
blue, the whole had the appearance of a rich piece of
jewelry, more dazzling than the crosses that emperors
sometimes wear as decorations in their buttonholes. It

21

was all so wonderfully beautiful, whether they seemed
to float in the sky —

> "Like pale rose chaplets or like sapphire mist, —
> Or hang or droop along the heavenly ways
> Like scarves of amethyst!"

"Come," said Puck, as Joy seemed inclined to waste
too much time over the cobwebs. "At this rate of
getting along, we shall never see the animals."

"What do you mean?" asked Joy. "Is the sky-
garden like the Zoölogical in London? do you keep
wild beasts here?"

"Look and see," replied Puck; and Joy uttered a
scream of fright as she saw coiling toward her an immense sea-serpent, while bears, lions, leopards, lynxes,
bulls, dragons, and other monsters followed in its
wake.

"Don't be afraid," said Puck: "they are only the constellations. And here we are at the zodiac; this is the
most interesting part of the garden, because each of
these great flower-beds has a fascinating mythological
story connected with it, which I will tell you, if you
choose, as we walk through. They were the fairy-stories

of the Greeks. I have no doubt Alcibiades had them told to him when he was a little boy. Some of the legends are a great deal older still. I should not wonder if Pharaoh's daughter, when she wished to steal away the heart of her little adopted son, told them —

'"Mongst the bulrushes to little Moses
Way down on the banks of the Nile;'

for the Egyptians gave the names to the constellations of the zodiac, twenty-five hundred years before the birth of Christ."

Joy knew the names: her father had taught them to her by means of a very old rhyme, which she now repeated : —

"The ram, the bull, the heavenly twins,
And next the crab the lion shines,
The virgin and the scales,
The scorpion, archer, and the goat,
The man who holds the watering-pot,
The fish with glittering tails."

As she approached nearer, she was surprised and pleased to find that they were not live animals, after all, but

23

only flower-beds laid out in these varied shapes; and
the star-flowers that grew in them were quite similar to
those in the other parts of the sky-garden. Joy asked
their names, and was told that they were sunflowers.
She was a little surprised at this; for they did not in the
least resemble the sunflowers on her grandfather's farm
in Vermont. She was very anxious to have Puck begin
his fairy-tales; and, after some urging, he did commence
one on the constellation of the ram, which promised to
be very interesting; when she felt her mother shaking
her vigorously by the shoulder, and heard her say that
every one had finished breakfast, that Bobby Copernicus
had eaten up all the waffles, and if she did not hurry she
would be late to school. Joy burst into tears: she could
have borne the loss of the waffles, but she had lost the
stories too. Night after night, she hoped and longed
that Puck would come again; but he did not. And
when she sat in the evening with her father and Uncle
Briar, on the observatory roof, the stars looked far away
and mysterious: all their brilliant coloring seemed to
have faded out. The constellations were not distinct, as
they were in the sky-garden, but had some way jumbled
themselves together; so that it was hard to tell where

one began and another left off. Uncle Briar had studied in Germany and in Paris, and now her father was trying to make an astronomer of him. Joy liked him very much, he was so gay and kind; and she wondered if he knew the stories of the zodiac. She felt sure that, if he did, he would tell them to her. And so one night when he was sitting up in the observatory waiting for an eclipse which would not be on for an hour or two, and Cousin Myrtle had gone up to keep him from being lonely, Joy woke Bobby Copernicus; and the two crept up the narrow stair in their nightgowns, and ran to where their pet uncle and cousin were sitting.

"You bad children! what did you come here for?" said Cousin Myrtle, taking them both in her lap, and wrapping them warmly in her soft gray shawl.

Then Joy told her dream, and how much she wanted to hear the stories of the zodiac. When she spoke of its all seeming so much plainer and more natural in the sky-garden than here upon the earth, Cousin Myrtle repeated softly, —

> " And the wonder of wonders is to me,
>   That the stars should nightly seem
>   Only a mystery in fact, —
>   A reality in dream ! "

25

"I should love dearly to please you, children," said Uncle Briar; "and if you can get mamma's permission to listen to them, I think Cousin Myrtle and I can tell you some tales of the zodiac which will perhaps interest you as much as those that your little friend Puck would have told. We will have one every evening. The first shall be for Joy; and Joy, I know, would like a romance best, — something about brave knight and lady fair and the Crusades; would she not?"

"But can I have my choice?" asked Joy.

"These stories shall be made to order," replied Uncle Briar. "And, since Joy does not object, we will begin the first one."

Part I.

TALES OF THE ZODIAC.

HE cluster of stars called the Constellation of the Ram was so named by the Greeks, from the old fable of the Golden Fleece. The ancients believed that far away in the land of Colchis the fleece of this ram was hung upon a tree guarded by a dragon. Jason went in search of it in a ship called the "Argo;" and, being helped by the daughter of the king of the island, the beautiful Medea,

29

he killed the dragon and carried away not only the golden fleece, but Medea too.

In the fourteenth century, when so many chivalric organizations were formed, one of the orders of knight-hood was that of the Toison d'Or, or Golden Fleece. There stands now in France, not very far from Paris, an old château built by a knight of this order, after he returned from fighting the infidels in the Holy Land. His portrait hangs in the great hall, and over it a coat-of-mail which they say was worn by the old crusa-der. The château is called the Falcon's Nest. There are magnificent avenues running through the hunting-grounds, a beautiful gate of forged iron, and a deep moat. In the family chapel the light falls through glorious old stained windows, the vivid violet and scarlet flaming on the damp stone pavement until they almost warm it. The saints in these gorgeous robes have, for the most part, faces cracked and patched and time-discolored, and are not very beautiful; but if you half close your eyes, so as not to see the forms, but only the color, the effect is very brilliant. The whole furnishing of the château resem-bled the chapel in that it was very magnificent and old and uncomfortable. It was filled with staircases, short

30

and narrow: there was no handsome flight that ran from hall to roof, but every room seemed built at a different elevation from the ground, and you could not pass from one to the other without stumbling up or down a few steps. There were no carpets; the dark hardwood floors were waxed till they reflected all the long slender legs of the furniture, and until it was a difficult matter to walk upon them. The hall that contained the portrait of Toison d'Or, as the servants called the old knight, was seventy feet square, and was meagrely furnished with chairs and tables and mirrors placed against the wall, while the centre of the room was left vacant, as though cleared for a dance or for a funeral. The only homelike spot in it was the oriel window, where Madame sat with a crimson Turkey rug under her feet, a table filled with bright house-plants at one side, and a basket of many-colored worsteds at the other, from which she continually embroidered fire-screens and chair-covers of nondescript and hideous pattern, sometimes of no pattern at all, — mere dashes and splashes of pleasantly contrasting hues. She called them church windows; and their effect was similar to that which I have described in the old chapel. A bright, pleasant little woman was Madame, with her very black eyes under her very white hair. She would have been a very happy woman, if it had not been for Gaston. Gaston was her only child, and the pride and torment of her life. In the first place, since he had come of age he insisted on living in Paris, and only came to the château in the hunting season, with some of his wild companions. Madame did not care to live in Paris; besides, Gaston did not need her there, and the old place did. Her thrifty oversight took the place of a man of affairs. There was a large farm connected with the château, and from it and the forest came the revenues of the family. They would have been ample too, but living in Paris was so expensive, and all the money went to Gaston: nothing was left for improvements, new tools and buildings and animals; and so the magnificent place was gradually going to decay, and it no longer brought in as much money as in former years. There was a great mortgage on it, too, which there was no hope of ever paying; and Madame prayed that the settlement might only not come in her day: Gaston would not very much care if the old place did go out of the name. But Gaston *did* care more than his mother knew. He was kind and noble at heart; but his good

qualities were crusted over by idleness and bad compan-
ionship. Down at the Grange the farmer and his family
believed in Gaston. They took good care of his hounds
that he loved so dearly; and Fifine, the farmer's daughter, said again and again, that all would be right if only
M. Gaston could be persuaded to give up Paris, and
live at the château.

One morning Baptiste, the house-servant, came down
in a great hurry. Fifine was needed at the château; for
there was to be company, among the rest some ladies,
and Fifine must act as maid while they remained.

The company was all in honor of the youngest guest,
—a golden-haired American girl, Miss Beatrice Rich,
familiarly called Betty, whose acquaintance Gaston had
made in Paris. Papa and Mamma Rich had been much
pleased with the young man; and when an invitation
came from Madame (at Gaston's request), to visit at the
château during the hunting-season, they complied with
a pleasure not unmixed with some curiosity, and half-
formed ambitious plans for Beatrice. Fifine was delighted with the young lady who rode so well, and whose
beautiful blonde hair floated in that semi-savage American way, below her slender waist. M. Gaston had chosen

33

a wife worthy of himself; and Fifine yielded her the homage of a true feudal vassal. One day the two girls stood alone before the portrait of Toison d'Or. "How much he resembles your master!" said Betty. "Do tell me who he was."

"He was one of M. Gaston's ancestors," replied Fifine, "a knight of the Golden Fleece. He killed four hundred Turks for the honor of the dear Christ and the Toison d'Or. M. Gaston is like him in character too; for I think he would do any thing for the Golden Fleece."

Miss Betty's brow clouded. "Do you mean," she asked, "that he would do any thing for money?"

"Ah, no, mademoiselle," said the girl impulsively. "I meant that mademoiselle's beautiful hair was like a golden fleece, and that M. Gaston would perform prodigies of valor for it, and— I wish I might say it; but no: that would be too bold."

"What was it you wished to say? You have begun with such a pretty compliment that I could forgive almost any thing now."

"I only meant that M. Gaston would do any thing mademoiselle wished; and if she would persuade him to give up his absinthe and his wild companions, and live all the year at the château, mademoiselle would make madame his mother and all of us very happy."

Betty Rich did not reply. She had often seen the young Frenchman seated at one of the little open-air tables in front of a fashionable restaurant in Paris, toying with a tall glass of whity-green absinthe, — a liquor very much in vogue in Paris, but worse in its effects than the vilest whiskey. They had tastes in common, which it would be very easy to cultivate together in this romantic spot. What if she could persuade him to give up idling on the boulevards, and devote his life to nobler purposes?

She had a long, serious talk with him that evening, as they rambled in the park. He was willing to leave Paris, he said, willing to live anywhere in the wide world, if only Betty would be his wife, and live there with him; but he could not see any harm in wine, and Betty seemed to him very unreasonable and fanatical to wish him to give it up. "Well, if I cannot make you see it as I do, Gaston," she had said at last, with tears in her eyes, "will you not give it up simply for love of me, granted that it is all right enough? Can you not deny yourself just a little because I wish it?"

35

Gaston was on the point of yielding; but he took her hand, and asked, "And you will not marry me if I refuse?"

Betty's lip quivered; but she answered firmly, "No, Gaston."

This was certainly a very different young lady from any he had ever met before. And Gaston's crooked European brain placed the situation before him in this way: here was a girl who preferred her own will to his pleasure, and was even willing to sacrifice her love for him, simply for the sake of having her own way.

"Then you cannot love me very much, Betty," he replied; and they entered the château with a great cloud of uncertainty and misunderstanding between them. The next day Gaston passed hunting with Mr. Rich; and in the evening there was a grand dinner, a number of his friends having driven out from Paris, and several of the neighboring families having been invited to share in the hospitalities of the mansion. The table was spread in the great hall; and Beatrice sat opposite Gaston and the portrait of Toison d'Or, which loomed above him, dim and mysterious, into the gloom of the upper part of the high vaulted room; for the candles

36

were all clustered in many-branched candelabra upon the table. The resources of the cellars of Falcon's Nest seemed inexhaustible; for, between the many courses, bottle after bottle of costly wines, with illustrious names, and corks bearing dates farther back than the Riches could trace their pedigree, were opened, and filled the variously shaped glasses that were grouped about the plate of each guest. Every gem with which Betty was familiar, except the blue-tinted ones, was represented: there was deep amber, rosy ruby, pale straw-colored topaz; liquors flashing and colorless as diamond, and deeply purple as amethyst. Baptiste filled her glasses once; and, though he was sent to her frequently with some rare old bottle reposing carefully in its wicker reclining-chair, he always found the glasses as he had left them,—full. Gaston noticed this circumstance from across the table. "You do not like our European wines, Mlle. Beatrice?" he asked. "Ah, well, you shall have something to remind you of home,—a drink which some Americans introduced to our club last winter, and which I am ashamed not to have already offered you. It is *ponch au rhum*, a very aristocratic beverage, so they tell me, in your

37

country. — Baptiste, bring me a decanter of the best old rum."

Beatrice hardly knew whether to be amused at the droll change of name which rum-punch had undergone in its passage across the ocean, or to be indignant at the assertion that it was a fashionable drink in America, when she was struck by something peculiar in Baptiste's behavior. The valet shrugged his shoulders, and declared that it was impossible.

"How impossible?" asked Gaston. "Do you mean to tell me that that barrel of rum is gone already?"

"No, *m'sieu*," replied Baptiste meekly; "but the cellars have been wet ever since the inundations, and we keep the wine now in the family tomb in the park. Since all of *m'sieu's* ancestors are removed to the cemetery, it seemed too bad not to make the stone vault of use; but though there are no longer any dead people there, *m'sieu* knows that to-morrow is the *Jour des Morts*, and that to-morrow is already here, for it is now past midnight. The dead are out; and, very like, some of them, being so used to the old tomb, may mistake their way home. I brought up all the wines that I thought could be used this afternoon; for I would not go to the vault — no, not if *m'sieu* would give me all that it contains."

Gaston laughed, and the company followed his example; but Beatrice thought she discovered beneath the noisy merriment an under-current of nervousness. *Jour des Morts* was All Saints' Day: the evening before corresponded with our Halloween; and the French are very superstitious in their observance of it.

"It is a fine joke," said Gaston, after the laughter had subsided; "for the wine which we are drinking now is an old acquaintance of my grandfather, the last who was laid to rest in the old tomb. He kissed the girls at its vintage, I have not a doubt. And the first for whom the sepulchre was reared, the chevalier whose portrait hangs above my head, regarded every flagon as a holy grail. They were all deep drinkers, all generous hosts: they ought to make a company of choice spirits. Gentlemen, I rise to propose their healths. — And now, Baptiste, give me the keys, and I will go for the liquor myself. As a family, we have doubtless many darker sins; but there is not a taint of cowardice in the whole line."

Beatrice smiled at this rather grandiloquent address, and rose from the table at the same time with Gaston, endeavoring to dissuade him from his freak. But the young man's pride was aroused, and he set out with a great appearance of courage. A half-hour, an hour passed; and still he did not return. After another interval, some of the bravest of the company, headed by Mr. Rich, went in search of him. They found him stretched in a fit upon the floor of the vault; and the next morning the young man related a wild ghost-story of how the bottles greeted him as he entered, saying that they contained the spirits of his forefathers; and, when he pooh-poohed at such nonsense, explained it philosophically, saying that lovers in this world become so completely identified as to exchange not their hearts alone, but their souls; that the process of assimilation was carried on by mind, as well as body; souls grew good by absorption, and the mind took its tint from the body's food. "And so," added the ghosts, "we gained our daily inspiration and mental force from the bottle; and now, instead of spirits of rectitude, we are all turned into rectified spirits of wine."

Mr. Rich shook his head gravely when he heard the account. He was not a man of strict habits himself; but a son-in-law with a tendency toward delirium tremens was not to be desired. He gave the young man a long and earnest talk, which, in the light of the event of the past night, had more effect upon Gaston's mind than Betty's arguments. He was the first to broach the subject when next they met, professing himself ready to make any promise that she wished. They were standing before the portrait of old Toison d'Or; a sheet of paper lay on a writing-table just beneath; and, seating herself beside it, Betty drew up a new oath of knight-errantry such as the " new crusade " in our own country battled for; and, when she left the room, it was with a temperance-pledge bearing Gaston's name in her pocket, and a betrothal ring upon her finger.

Betty's fortune repaired the old château, and put the farm into fine working order; but it was Gaston's talent, energy, and faithfulness to his pledge, that carried it forward so successfully, and inspired so much confidence in him in the minds of his neighbors, that, the next time he visited Paris, it was as member of the Corps Légis-latif.

The old green dragon of absinthe was slain, and the Golden Fleece was won.

" I don't call *that* much of a story," said Bobby Copernicus contemptuously, as Uncle Briar ended his recital.
" It may do well enough for girls; but it isn't a bit the
style that boys like.   Love-stories just make me sick.
I want something about fighting Injuns or bears or
something, or a regular staving good story about pirates
and snakes and things.   I should think you might tell
a story on purpose for me this time.   Come, now : won't
you ? "

" A fighting spirit is a very good one," said Uncle
Briar, " provided you fight for something worth fighting
for.   We have need of warriors and heroes nowadays;
and as our next constellation is that of the bull, and
seems to suggest something belligerent, I will try to
tell Bobby a story to-morrow night, of something that
happened in Spain.   It is the story of a boy with tastes
somewhat like Bobby's.

I T was not at all like *your* father's umbrella, with the carved ivory handle, respectable black silk cover, and neat oilskin case; nor a dainty little *en tout cas* like the one at Maud's silver chatelaine; nor a huge white canvas sketching-umbrella such as Cousin Fred, the artist, takes with him to the Adirondacks. Neither was it exactly like Grandfather Prendergast's blue gingham, nor the bamboo affair with which Wah Lee the Chinese laundryman protects his pigtail upon state occasions. Father Zenobe's was claret-color, bordered with five white lines. It was considered a very sober and steady-going affair; for in Spain the priests, who love bright colors as much as other Spaniards, make up for their black robes by the gayest possible umbrellas.

Father Zenobe's was only a rich, dark dahlia, compared to the gorgeous tropical flowers which blossomed over the heads of some of his brother-priests. Father Ignatius could be seen of an afternoon, strolling along the seashore, laughing and chatting with all he met, under a bright yellow one with pale blue lining. Father Pedro's was rose-color lined with yellow; and when standing on the town-wall, with the setting sun behind him, he looked like a picture of one of the old saints with a glory about his head. Father Sebastian generally appeared with an assortment of walking-sticks and umbrellas under his arm, so that he presented a striking resemblance to his patron saint in the church paintings, — all bristling with arrows. They were all priests, *curés* at the church of Fontarabia, just over the border-line from France, the most northern seaport town of Spain, — picturesque old Fontarabia, as seen from French territory, with its crumbling walls from twenty to thirty feet in thickness, its ruined castle, and church with beautiful semi-Moorish cupola. It stands upon a promontory, the sandy shoals of the Bidassoa in front, and the sea shimmering away to the west, seemingly an enchanted isle. Nor is a walk in the streets of the old town less bewitching. They are very narrow, and the houses very high, a balcony running along the front of each story. Sometimes these balconies have balustrades of forged iron in beautiful lace-like tracery; sometimes they are of carved wood: whatever the material, they are always brilliant with color, — pots and boxes of gay flowers, bird-cages, rugs, and strips of bright carpeting hung over the railing, dark-eyed ladies in still more dazzling costumes; and, as if this were not bright enough, the very walls of the houses painted in stripes, drab and pink, white and green, and deep red. The most interesting spot in this most interesting town is the old church. It is one of the few fortified churches to be found in Europe. As you enter the door, you are startled: you almost think you have lost your way; for, instead of shrine or confessional, you find yourself confronted by the grim loop-holes of a stone barricade. In this church, with its walls covered with rich maroon and gilding tarnished to the right degree of artistic dinginess, Father Zenobe said the masses for the dead, and heard the boys say their catechism. He loved the boys, though he had small cause to do so; for a dirtier or more idle set, except where mischief was concerned, could not be found in all Spain, playing their pranks even in the old church, and on Father Zenobe himself. Nor was the other part of his vocation a cheerful one; and yet the happy old priest preferred his duties to those

45

of any of his brothers. He would never have exchanged them with Father Sebastian, who did the christening; for his bright street boys were so much more interesting than the blinking, spasmy babies, who shuddered and shrieked in such heretic fashion when the Church received them into its bosom; or with Father Pedro, who performed the marriage ceremony. It was always a severe trial for Father Zenobe, when, as it sometimes happened, away on the church's business, he was called upon to do this: the sweet, flushed faces of the brides recalled to memory an early hope laid on the altar of Mother Church. Not for worlds would he have heard the confessions, like Father Ignatius (the recitals of sin and frailty were too heart-rending); or administered the last communion and visited the sick, like Father Francisco. It was all very well, rather cheerful than otherwise, he would have told you, to do what he could to rest people's souls after they were dead; but he had a sympathetic heart, and the sight of human suffering and death wrung it sorely. A genial, easy-going man at this time was Father Zenobe. He used to say of himself, that he resembled Spain's greatest painter in two things: he loved the Madonna and ragged street-boys. Wilder and more ragged than any *gamin* that Murillo ever painted, was Fadrique Zuloaga. He was Father Zenobe's favorite, for he was brighter and gayer than the others, though he was always foremost in scrapes, and determined to learn as little as possible of the catechism, for the simple reason that his parents had destined him to the Church; and Fadrique had determined in his rebellious little heart that he would be as wicked as ever he could, so as not to be fit for a priest. Father Zenobe taught the boys to sing, as well as to repeat the catechism; and on state occasions, robed in pretty lace overskirts and scarlet dresses, they would roar out the church canticles while they held the candles and banners, censers and crucifixes. Fadrique was always grimacing and joking on such occasions; but he sang with the rest because he had an ear for music, and some way the song would roll out in spite of him. Sometimes he liked the words too, they were so odd and quaint. I will give you an almost literal translation of some of the verses of a Christmas carol which was one of Fadrique's favorites, because it was always acted in pantomime, and Fadrique loved acting even better than singing : —

" He was born in a hovel
    Of spider-webs full :
Beside Him there grovel
    An ox and a mule ;
And King Melchior bade,
    To honor the day,
And that none might be sad,
    The musicians should play.

" I'm a poor little gypsy
    From over the sea :
I bring him a chicken
    That cries '*quir-i-qui ;*'
For each of us, sure,
    Should offer his part :
Be you ever so poor,
    You can give him your heart.

" Good night, Father Joseph !
    Madonna so mild,
We leave with regret
    Your adorable child,
With the crown on his locks,
    The symbol of rule :
Sleep in peace, Señor Ox !
    God bless you, Sir Mule ! "

48

Fadrique loved the good priest; and so, despite his hatred of the Church, he remained with him, studying and singing, until he was nearly old enough to take clerical orders. Then one day he suddenly disappeared; and his father came to Father Zenobe with the intelligence that Fadrique had run away with a company of *torreros*, or bull-fighters.

The old man looked grave; for the news made him sore at heart. "This is because we were trying to force him into the Church," said he. "If you want to serve God with a child, you must let him become what God has fitted him to be. Now, Fadrique is no more fitted to be a bull-fighter than he is to be a priest: he has always wanted to be a sailor. And you know, we Basques have a proverb, 'If a man does not know how to pray, let him go to sea, and the storms will teach him.'"

"All that may be very true," said Fadrique's father; "and I had certainly rather that my son should be a sailor than the most skilful *picador* that ever worried a bull. But you should have told me this before: it seems to me that it is too late now."

"Perhaps not," said Father Zenobe.

49

After this occurrence the good priest developed a strange taste for bull-fighting. He sat long in the little tobacco-shops, reading the newspapers; and he never seemed to read any thing but notices of entertainments of this kind. He bought all the bills and programmes that were offered him, no matter at what place the combat was to take place. He had long conversations with people who made it their business to bet on the event of such combats; and altogether one would have thought that the reverend gentleman was developing very unclerical tastes. It was about a year after this, that a bull-fight was announced for the festival of St. Ignatius at Loyola. As this is one of the principal religious fête-days in Spain, Father Zenobe obtained permission to attend, without difficulty. It was not a very singular thing to see priests at bull-fights. At Loyola was situated one of the most magnificent convents in all Spain; and the entertainments held here on the festival of St. Ignatius were always under the especial patronage of the Church. Among the gayly dressed *banderilleros* who exposed their lives that day in the arena, was a slender boy, dressed in a tightly fitting suit of delicate green satin, with flesh-colored stockings, gold ornaments, and a rose-colored sash. Father Zenobe knew him by his curly head, and the dash and bravado of his bearing. He was the youngest combatant, and seemed to be a special favorite with the audience and with the troupe ; for the former showered down cigars and bouquets at each daring exploit, and the latter shielded him as much as possible, keeping him away from the more dangerous parts of the field. Father Zenobe had taken one of the high-priced seats usually reserved for the "fancy," or professional connoisseurs at bull-fights, in the front row. The awning that covered the audience in the higher tiers did not shade him, and he sat exposed to the rays of the summer sun. At first he had cautiously raised his beloved umbrella ; but he had been obliged to close it instantly, some of the audience objecting even to his long, skiff-shaped, black hat, as too much obstructing the view. The spectacle, with all its horror of blood and brutality, had gone on for some time; and now the moment had arrived for Fadrique's feat. Seated in a chair in the centre of the arena, he was to fix a little dart in each side of the bull's neck as it charged toward him. The animal was a huge creature, black as a coal, with a small fiery eye. A garnet ribbon, which indicated to whose drove he belonged, was fastened to one horn, and ran trickling down the middle of his forehead like a rill of blood. He advanced slowly toward Fadrique, as though curious to know why he was sitting. When he had reached the proper distance, Fadrique raised both arms, and threw the darts with all his force into the bull's flesh; then the creature, maddened by the pain, lunged suddenly forward; and something was tossed again and again from his horns into the air. It was only the chair; for Fadrique had saved himself by an agile leap to one side, and was now standing in a statuesque attitude with folded arms, seemingly indifferent to the plaudits that rang around the arena. But he was too careless: the bull discovered in a moment that the chair was not his real enemy, and tossed Fadrique just as, off his guard, he was replying to the audience with a graceful bow. He fell heavily, not far from the spot where Father Zenobe was sitting. There happened to be no attendants in this part of the field, and the bull was approaching with lowered horns. Fadrique lay completely in his power, when a red meteor shot through the air, and diverted the animal's attention. It was

52

Father Zenobe's great claret-colored umbrella, which he, with remarkable presence of mind and exactitude of aim, had thrown before the eyes of the angry bull. When, after the sport, it was handed to him again, two springs were broken, and its rich claret cover was stained with an angrier hue: thank Heaven it was not human blood! for in that brief interval some of the assistants had had time to drag Fadrique out of the bull's reach. His life was saved; but a leg was broken, and it would be necessary for him to give up his new profession for a long time. Father Zenobe had him carried carefully back to Fontarabia, and nursed him with true paternal care through his long convalescence. At length, when it was evident that he had almost recovered, and would soon have the use of his limb as before, he bade him good-by. "I shall not be able to attend every bull-fight," said he; "but I shall pray to Our Lady to shield you from all danger."

Fadrique's eyes filled with tears: "I have had enough of bull-fighting," he said; "and if you wish it I will be a priest."

"I do not wish it," replied the wise old man; "but I have your father's permission for you to go to sea: you

53

will have nobler opportunities for daring there than in the bull-ring, and can, if you choose, serve God as truly as in the cloister."

And so Fadrique became a sailor on the stormiest of waters, — a fisherman of the Bay of Biscay. On his return from his first voyage he hung as a votive offering, before the picture of Christ walking upon the sea, in the old church of Fontarabia, a model of his ship; such as are common in Spanish churches, as mementos of rescues from shipwreck, and which sway like pendulums from long cords attached to the ceiling. Father Zenobe was right: he did not know how to pray, but the storms had taught him. They have taught him more; for, in the most terrible gales that drive the surf high upon this formidable coast, there is no one more active in fitting out the life-boat for the rescue of those in distress than Fadrique. He is as reckless as ever, and counts his life as little worth, if only he may lay it down in a cause that is really worthy.

54

GEMINI

ELIJAH'S RAVENS

"HE raven, though an unclean bird, brought food to Elijah."

The words were those of the celebrated missionary, Dr. William Goodell. Sallie had heard Miss Dibbs read them long ago; but they came back to her with new force to-day. "If ebber dar war a prophet ob de Lord," she muttered to herself, "Miss Dibbs is dat ar. An' if ebber dar war two ornery brack crows, dem ar's Praise an' me."

Praise was Sallie's twin brother. Their mother — a very pious old negress, who did Miss Dibbs's washing — had named her children Praise and Salvation; and, dying a few years before the beginning of this story, had left them both, twelve years of age, as a legacy to Miss Dibbs. Sallie's mother had experienced so many kindnesses from Miss Dibbs's hand, that she was not to blame for thinking her the possessor of considerable wealth; but she was, in reality, an industrious, economical little old lady, who found it hard work enough to make her accounts square on each Saturday night. She had a tiny room in the upper story of a second-class boarding-house, on a shady street in New York City. It was up so high that the sun could peep in and cheer up the cosey little apartment, with the geraniums in the window, the canary in its cage, and the old-fashioned painted tea-set on the rack against the wall. There were many bright spots of color in the room, which rendered it remarkably cheery, and gave it a right to the name of Cherith, which Miss Dibbs had conferred upon it one day when she was particularly lonesome, and could compare herself to no one but Elijah in the desert.

And now the ravens had come too. Miss Dibbs would not have known what to do with them if she had not received that very day another legacy of several thousand dollars from an early friend. There was no excuse for her now. She was quite independent, and could live comfortably on the income of her money: no need to make pincushions and tidies for the fancy-stores any longer; and she accepted both legacies with thankfulness. She determined to devote her leisure time to instructing Sallie in sewing and in the line of work which she had herself pursued, hoping thus to make the child self-supporting. But what to do with Praise? This was indeed a problem. She had visions of giving him a theological education, and sending him as a missionary to christianize Africa. But Praise soon showed her that, in spite of his name, he was a most irreligious youth. He occupied Miss Dibbs's coal-closet with great delight at night, and by day roamed the streets with the utmost freedom. "I will consult the child's taste," said Miss Dibbs to herself, "and try to help him forward in any career in life which he may have chosen for himself." And Praise, when asked what he would like to be when he grew up, replied, with intense enthusiasm, "A brakeman!"

Miss Dibbs had just invested her money in railway shares, and listened to the boy's preference with more leniency than she otherwise might. By dint of many calls at offices, she obtained for him the position of night sub-porter, on a train leaving New York at ten o'clock, and arriving at Grimy Junction early in the morning.

He had charge of the boot-blacking department, and was generally the slave of stalwart Mose, who wore the silver label on his cap that proclaimed him the proper person to receive fees from passengers for this same boot-blacking and other services executed by Praise. At Grimy Junction, Praise swallowed a cup of coffee, and sprang on board a returning freight-train, reaching New York about noon, and at once coiled himself up to sleep in Miss Dibbs's coal-closet.

Once Miss Dibbs took a trip on the owl-train. "I shall feel perfectly safe," were her good-night words to Praise, as she carefully held the curtains together beneath her nose, — " I shall feel perfectly safe, because you have charge of the train."

Praise perched himself on the wood-box, · with his arms hugging his knees, and waited for the conductor to make his last round. It was a perfect night, and he meant to spend it upon the rear platform; but he knew that if the conductor found him there he would kick him; and so he sagaciously bided his time. He loved to sit there, with his eyes fixed upon the brilliant crimson lantern. To Praise, it was a glorious ruby pendent from the ear of his lady-love; for he had learned to love the owl-train, and its swift dashing through the night.

Praise had dozed upon the platform for several hours, when he woke suddenly to a consciousness of something wrong. He was slow of thought, but it came to him at last, — the lantern was gone! The train was running along the river-bank, on piles that carried the track out over the water. A fog had come up from the river, hiding every object; and the danger-signal was not in its place: it had probably been insecurely fastened, and dropped off. His first impulse was to go and tell Mose, when straight out of the blackness there blazed upon him a sun, — the head-light of a rapidly approaching locomotive. Praise danced and shrieked in terror, but the engineer neither saw nor heard; and the next sensation that he experienced was that of flying rapidly through the air, and landing suddenly in the soft mud, covered with yellow water-lilies, on the landward side of the track. He picked himself up entirely uninjured, and waded back to the train. The last car lay upon its side in the water. "Number six," said he to himself, counting the windows, and bursting in the blinds of one of them by frequent applications of his head in the style of a battering-ram. Through this opening he drew out little Miss Dibbs fainting with pain, and sadly injured. He staggered with her to shore, and sat holding her in his arms until the relief-train was made up to convey the wounded to the city. The physician who waited on the gentle lady the next morning said that she would never walk again, never stand or sit erect; for her spine was incurably injured. She did not suffer very much, but lay with a cheerful smile on her sweet face; and Sallie waited and tended upon her most devotedly.

"It isn't as bad as it might be," said the uncomplaining little lady. "I can afford to be sick. My income comes every month, without any exertion on my part. I am one of God's broken-winged sparrows; and he always takes care of them."

It was now, too, that Miss Dibbs took real comfort in her other legacy, the twins. To her many thanks Sallie's unfailing reply was, "Clar to goodness, Miss Dibbs, I only wish I could do mo'."

Her wish was gratified sooner than she thought. Late one night, after extra work at the bank, Mr. St. Ledger, the pleasant-faced old gentleman who usually brought Miss Dibbs her crisp new bills in a great yellow envelope, appeared before the astonished child, and with a distressed look, and a nervous rubbing of his hands, inquired for her mistress.

"Her back powerful bad to-day, sah, and she done gone to bed," replied Sallie.

"Perhaps you can communicate the news as well," said the old gentleman, with a start of relief. "The company in which Miss Dibbs's funds were invested has utterly failed. I have been able to save nothing, absolutely nothing. You will please tell her how much it pains me to be the bearer of such tidings." And, with a bow, the little old gentleman was gone.

Sallie entered her mistress's room. How peacefully she slept! As she watched her, the tears welled up into her great eyes. She turned, and sat down upon the rug before the grate, holding her head between her hands, gripping savagely into her woolly hair as she rocked to and fro. She was thinking out a plan of her own. "She sha'n't nebber know it. Praise and me'll fix it." And so they did; for the next morning Sallie went the rounds of the fancy-stores where Miss Dibbs had been known, and obtained a quantity of dolls to dress for the approaching holidays, together with orders for needle-books, pincushions, and tidies, enough to keep her at work for a whole year. But Sallie did not intend to do a stitch of this work. She knew plenty of needy girls and women out of employment, who would be glad to do it for her at a less price than the shopkeepers had offered. Her next work was to visit the fashionable dressmakers, and for a trifling price buy up pieces and remnants of silk and other goods, which she distributed among her workwomen. Her scheme progressed finely. Miss Dibbs imagined that Sallie was attending school; and as she only went out in the afternoon, when Praise could take her place, her mistress did not lack for attention. The boy helped with his earnings too; and at the close of the month, when they counted them over in the coal-closet, they found they had a few pennies more than Miss Dibbs's monthly income.

Praise took a little heap of currency, and had it changed into larger and newer bills. Then he bought an envelope like Mr. St. Ledger's; and, when Sallie presented it to her mistress, the good lady had no idea but that it was her rightful due.

This went on throughout the winter; but, when the stifling summer came, Miss Dibbs grew tired of her upper room with its continual glare, and made the announcement to the horrified Sallie that she intended to pass a month at Saratoga. " I find that I can board there as cheaply as here," she said. " I shall buy a great reclining-chair : you can wheel me about, and perhaps the water will do me good. I will write a note to Mr. St. Ledger to send my remittances there."

There was nothing to be said. Sallie explained her work to Praise, and asked him to carry it on during her absence. The boy did his best; but he was not as successful as Sallie, and at the close of the month he lacked several dollars of the required amount. He walked bravely to the bank, and asked Mr. St. Ledger to lend him the sum. Deeply touched by this simple story of love and devotion, Mr. St. Ledger made out a check, and, enclosing with it a short business note, addressed the whole in his well-known hand to Miss Dibbs. " After this, come to me every month, my boy," said he. " Let me make it up whenever it falls short, and bring it regularly as I used to."

Mr. St. Ledger came, but not as he used to. His visits were more frequent than business required; and as he sat in pleasant room " Cherith," watching the sweet-faced woman reclining on the crimson couch, her silvery curls peeping from under a dainty cap with fresh lavender ribbons, his sympathy grew more and more unbounded. And so it happened that the minister came with him one evening, and Miss Dibbs was changed to Mrs. St. Ledger. Little room "Cherith" spread itself out into an entire flat, about which Sallie wheeled her mistress with infinite delight. Mr. St. Ledger often says in joke, that he married his wife for her money; and she retorts pleasantly, that he shall never have a penny of it, for she intends to leave it all to the twins. She means it too, good lady; for to this day she believes herself independent in fortune, and does not know how for many months she was supported by "Elijah's Ravens."

S O you wish one of my war experiences (said Uncle Briar to the children the next evening). As it happens, there was one which might have happened under the constellation of the Crab. It was in the month of June, 1861, that Gen. Butler sent a party from Fortress Monroe to fortify a point called Newport News at the mouth of the James River. I formed one of the expedition. We had remained here for some time, when my commanding officer thought it necessary to communicate with Gen. Butler, and despatched me with written documents to Fortress Monroe. I started alone, and on foot. The attempt was a hazardous one; and I came very near falling into the hands of a troop of Confederate cavalry. But evening found me safe at the little town of Hampton, overlooked by the frowning walls of the fortress.

Its population had been so disloyal that out of a thousand inhabitants there now remained but one hundred who avowed themselves Unionists, and claimed Gen. Butler's protection.

I had intended to go directly on; but the night promised to be a stormy one, and I concluded to pass it at Hampton. The hotel was closed; and selecting a large hospitable-appearing mansion, I asked if I could obtain shelter for the night. A tall, brilliant-appearing Southern girl heard my request, and saying, "I will see," gave me a seat in the hall, and vanished. I was not its only occupant. A ragged little darkey sat upon the lower step of the grand staircase, amusing himself by training a crab. He held in his hand a ball of kite-twine, the end of which was attached to one of the creature's claws. As he unrolled this, the crab ambled briskly down the hall, guided in its movements by sundry twitches and tugs at the line, accompanied by such exclamations as, "Gee! Whoa dar! Keep de road, sinnah! Go for true, dar. Keep a steady trot. We don't want no 'lopin' nor canterin' on dis yere race-course."

In spite of my weariness, I found myself much interested in this queer performance. "What is your name, my boy?" I asked.

"Gen. Lee Beauregard Jefferson Davis," he replied.

"That is a suspicious name," I thought, "for an occupant of a Union family."

"Crabs is mighty knowin'," continued the boy. "I let dis one hab de whole run of dis yere ball ob twine, and den I winds him up again. One day when I began to wind, it didn't come easy; an' de next minute my marm done pumped him out ob de cistern. Clar to goodness, massa, if dis yere crab hadn't clomb up de chimney, slumped 'long de roof into de eaves-spout, flop down into de cistern, an den come up tru de pump. If you don't belicbe me, just look at dat knot in my kite-string; dat's where I bust it befo' I ebber got it straightened out."

I had not time to object to the improbability of the story; for the young lady whom I had before seen now appeared, and introduced her mother, a dignified, handsome woman, who welcomed me cordially to the hospitalities of the mansion. At the supper-table, the younger lady appeared remarkably nervous and excited, starting at the least sound, eating nothing, and taking no part in the conversation. Even her mother, although perfectly polite, seemed a trifle absent-minded.

Suddenly there was a heavy tread upon the veranda, and a loud, familiar knock at the door. The daughter sprang from her seat, overturning it, and sped away into the hall, closing the door behind her. My hostess made no remark at the conduct of her daughter, and entertained me agreeably throughout the meal, with only a little spot of heightened color on either cheek to tell of any agitation she might have felt. Nothing remarkable happened during the evening; and I was shown into a spacious chamber opening upon a hall that branched in two directions, and was well lighted by large windows through which the moonlight streamed; for the threatening storm had cleared away, and I had a vague feeling that perhaps I ought even now to continue my journey. But tired nature prevailed, and I was soon fast asleep. I was awakened by a scratching and shuffling noise in my room, for which I was for some time at a loss to account. I sat up in bed, and looked and listened, and at length discovered a small object on the uncarpeted floor, just passing over the door-sill into the hall. It was Gen. Lee Beauregard Stonewall Jackson's crab. " I will throw that nuisance out of the window!" I exclaimed, and sprang from my bed. The creature was out of my room; and I made a hasty half-toilet before following it. There it was at some distance down the hall; but, before reaching it, I heard some one mounting the staircase, and under the impulse of the moment I stepped into a room which, through its open door, I saw to be unoccupied. From behind this door, I could have, unobserved, a view of the hall. It was the General himself, who had come up the stairs, and who now intruded his woolly head into my chamber. He made some strong expression of surprise, that was interrupted by the falling of a hand upon his collar, and a sudden facing about to meet the angry looks of his mistress, who, with her daughter, had come up from the other end of the hall.

" What do you mean by looking into a gentleman's room?" she exclaimed, in a stage whisper, shaking the boy violently with both hands.

" I was lookin' for my crab, missus," gasped the boy.

" You know that is not the truth," replied the lady.

"Go down to the kitchen; and to-morrow you shall have such a whipping!"

"Yes, missus," replied the boy submissively. But, the instant that he was released, he exclaimed, "Dar's my crab now!" sprang by my door, pocketed his property, and then obeyed his mistress's orders.

Mother and daughter walked down the hall, and stood together by the great window near the door behind which I was concealed.

"It is almost time they were here," said the mother: "it does not usually take so long to go and come from Little Bethel."

"Father said he would ride as fast as he could," replied the girl, "and bring back enough of the soldiers to secure his capture. Father thinks he may be the bearer of important despatches."

"We can only wait, my dear," replied the lady: "let us go down into the parlor. I have locked his door on this side; you may have the key to give to your papa, if you wish."

After they had gone, I found myself in a new dilemma. How was I to descend and leave the house, when the ladies were in a room commanding a view of the only staircase with which I was acquainted? While I stood hesitating in the hall, my foot struck a small white object; and, stooping, I found that I had the General's ball of kite-twine. Its end was probably attached to the crab. I walked slowly along, winding the ball as I went, and following the thread which stretched on before me, round an angle, through a narrower and more dimly lighted passage, and down a winding and uneven staircase which led me to a rear entrance to the house. The door was open; and the twine still led on to where, at the foot of the garden, the General was swinging on the gate.

"Here is your ball," I said to him, as his eyes protruded to their utmost in recognizing me.

As I passed on towards the shore, I heard some one running behind me. It was the General.

"Clar to goodness, massa!" said he, "my crab done lighted out for de salt water: shouldn't wonder if he foun' him in Pete's boat; he allers did like to go a-fishin' with Pete. He'd sit up on de side ob de boat, an' help him claw in de lines. I'll go an' fotch Pete."

Pete, a stalwart fisherman, readily agreed to take me across to the fortress in his boat.

71

"I'll go wid yer," said the General: "shouldn't wonder if my crab war ober dar: don't see him nowhar 'bout dis yere boat."

And a tacit agreement was immediately instituted between us, whereby the General became my faithful follower through the entire war, at the close of which he entered a school for freedmen, and is himself now a teacher of his race, remarkable for his integrity and love of truth.

Established in our new quarters at the fortress, as I poured out the water for my morning ablutions, I found the General's crab in my wash-basin.

"Done tole yer so, massa," said the boy. "Dis yere crab done swum across de bay: mose likely he was up dar at headquarters, an' hearn tell jus' whar he should find us."

"General, General!" I said, "if you are to stay with me, you must speak the truth." And so he did; for I never knew him to prevaricate in any instance, except when it concerned his crab.

"PLEASE, Cousin Myrtle, there isn't any such thing as ghosts, is there?" asked Bobby Copernicus, one evening.

"That depends," replied Myrtle.

"Coz I told Joy I was going to tease for a ghost-story to-night, — a regular scarer; like the kind the snark told, you know, —

'Till each man's blood
Up on end it stood,
And the hair ran cold in their veins.'

And Joy said she didn't want that kind: she's 'fraid of 'em."

"Only people who do wrong need be afraid of ghosts," said Cousin Myrtle; "and it is very seldom

73

that other people see them. If you ever do any thing mean or shameful, you may be sure that it will haunt you all your life; and you will never need a candle to see it in the darkest night. But good people can almost always sleep soundly, even after a supper of strawberry shortcake, and never see one of the hobble-de-goblins; and, even if they do, there are no lions in the way, that can hurt Mr. Greatheart. By the way, our constellation to-night is that of the Lion. Bobby shall have his wish; for I do not think Joy would have been a bit frightened by

THE GHOST AT THE WHITE LION.

In the little village of Pudsey-in-the-Mud, England, stands the comfortable, old-fashioned inn of the White Lion. It was a hostelry of style and importance, with no lack of patronage, when the London stage-line swept through Pudsey; but the new railroad had left the little town several miles one side, and there was now little in its appearance to suggest its former state. Only chance travellers stopped here now, strangers visiting Pudsey for the first time; for in spite of its large, airy chambers, its cosey sitting-room with the carved fireplace and red window-curtains, its garden overgrown with sweet, old-fashioned flowers, its cook noted for making the most melting pastry in the shire, its obliging landlord and low charges, the White Lion was shunned by summer boarders, and by all who knew its history; for no one, even in incredulous England, liked to stop at a haunted house; and the inn was haunted, not by one ghost alone, but by many. It seemed as if it was the house spoken of in the Scriptures, found empty, swept and garnished, by the evil spirit, who immediately filled it with a variety of occupants as evil as himself; for none of the ghosts told of by the lodgers at the White Lion bore any great resemblance to each other.

The landlord was not a man to be frightened out of his wits by such stories: he had never seen any ghosts in the house, and, if he had, he would not have cared very much, if they had only paid their bills like respectable boarders. But they were now so deeply in his debt, and had kept away more lucrative lodgers so long, that the thing was growing unbearable; and, as a last resort, he had asked the sheriff to serve them with a notice to quit. This he had neatly framed, and hung in the haunted chamber. It was the pleasantest room in the front part of the house, with a very large square window filled with very small diamond-shaped panes. A small brass rod ran across the lower part of this window, and from it hung a ruffled muslin curtain ; but the upper and larger part was not covered by blind or curtain or screen of any kind, and allowed the sunlight or moonlight to fall in a broad band upon the well-scoured floor. Outside the window, a narrow balcony ran ; but it had only been for ornament in its best days, as the window was not made to open ; and now no human being could have walked across it ; for the floor was gone, and nothing was left but the cast-iron railing. Over the balcony hung the sign of the house, a wooden lion in a defiant attitude, with his paws raised as though for a trial of skill in boxing, and a very long curly tail twisted into several impossible knots. The lion was suspended from an iron rod fastened into the house above the window, and for several years had bid defiance to the ghosts, and beckoned passing travellers in vain.

The last lodger who had seen an apparition here was a queer old gentleman from London. He seemed very rich, but was much out of health, and was accompanied

76

by a servant and a nurse who put him to bed as soon
as he arrived. At midnight he aroused the house by
ringing his bell violently. When the landlord entered
the room, he lay in a fit with his back to the window;
and, when he came out of it, could not be persuaded
to look in that direction. He said that he had seen a
spirit, a white lady, who glided along the floorless
balcony, and peered into the window. The nurse and
landlord could see nothing remarkable; but the vision
had made such a strong impression on the old gentleman's mind, that the next day he sent for a lawyer, and
made a new will. " The greater part of my fortune,"
he said, " belonged to my cousin Helen. I was her
guardian. It was all invested in a company that failed
dishonestly; but I had been shrewd enough to withdraw the money before the failure. No one knew of
this, however; for the company's books were burned by
a member of the firm, and Helen believed that her
fortune was lost. She is dead now. She lived all her
life in poverty, while I have been very rich. It was she
who came last night; she beckoned to me. I cannot
give her back her property, but I can leave all, hers and
mine, to her children; and this is why I wish to make

a new will." The old gentleman felt that his cousin would come again the next night, and that when he saw her he would die. But she did not appear: the night was a rainy one, and I believe no one ever saw a ghost with an umbrella; and the next day the old gentleman was so much better that he went back to London. He did not die for many years afterward, but he sought out his cousin's children, and made ample restitution. In spite of his great wrong, they grew to love him very tenderly, living with him and caring for him until he died.

This was the last ghost that had been seen at the White Lion, when one afternoon a traveller arrived who was to deliver a lecture that evening at the town-hall. To honor his guest, the landlord and his wife attended the lecture. It was a great piece of nonsense; for the poor man tried to prove that the Bible was not true, that there were no angels, no future life, no God. He gave many quotations from the Scriptures to prove their absurdity. He scoffed at the visions of Daniel, at the winged lion, at the beast with ten horns, and made a great many jokes about the creatures in the Revelation, especially those that were like horses prepared for battle, with crowns of gold on their heads, men's faces, women's hair, the teeth of lions, and tails like scorpions with terrible stings, and were commanded to hurt only those men who had not the seal of God in their foreheads.

When he returned to the inn, the landlord shook hands with him warmly. "You are just the person I have been wanting to see," he said. " I have a room in my house that they say is haunted. If you do not believe in the supernatural, you will not object to sleeping there; and it will be a great thing for me if you can assert afterward that the ghosts are all humbug."

The lecturer professed himself perfectly willing to make the experiment; but he showed the landlord a brace of loaded pistols, and warned him that if he saw any thing unusual during the night he should certainly fire at it. Then he ate a hearty supper of dumpling and Welsh rarebit, washed down with strong ale, and went to bed. It was a moonlight night, — just such a one as the ghost of the White Lion preferred for its rambles; and the landlord was not much surprised at being awakened, when the night was half over, by the rapid firing of his guest's pistols. After the shots, all was silent for a few moments; and then the lecturer came tumbling down the winding stairs, his face colorless with fright. "I take it all back!" he shrieked. "I will nail my recantation to the church doors, only let me off this time! let me off this time!"

"What's the matter?" asked the landlord, who was standing at the foot of the stairs with a lighted candle in his hand.

"I have seen it!" said the frightened man, trembling violently, and clutching his host's arm.

"Seen what?"

"The beast!"

"The fiddlesticks! you've been dreaming; you've had the nightmare; you are not awake yet. If you saw any beast, it was the ghost of that Welsh rarebit."

"I have not been asleep at all. The Prince of the Power of the Air has been banging every shutter about this ruinous old house, and yelling down the chimneys, in a way that would have made it impossible for any one to sleep, even if he had not believed in demons, and had supposed it was only the wind, as I did. Let me go into your tap-room, and lock the door well, and I will tell you all about it."

And the lecturer told how he had grown so nervous, what with the hearty supper and the wind, that he found it impossible to sleep; and finally sat up in bed, wondering if it really was the wind that made all that noise. Suddenly something flew slowly across the window: it was a dark object, and might have been a bat, if it had not been of such great size. He looked again, and the object returned, this time clearly defining its shape, that of a lion; but who had ever seen a lion fly in this way between heaven and earth? Suddenly he remembered the winged lion of Daniel, and the creature of the Revelation that he had so derided. Yes, this answered the description perfectly, even to the flowing feminine tresses, and the tail with the terrible stings. The beast seemed to be trying the window-sash; for it rattled fearfully as his claws approached now the upper and now the lower portion, now the right and now the left side. The lecturer aimed his pistols at the animal's head, and fired them together, shivering the glass. But the ghostly thing did not seem in the least troubled by the shots: it paused an instant, and regarded him with two luminous eyes that he had not noticed before, and then made a sudden swoop toward the broken casement, he did not stop to see with what success, for he knew that he had not the seal of God in his forehead.

It was a singular story, and reminded the landlord of the one told by an occupant of the room several months before. He was a suspicious-looking character, who carried a small black valise of which he was particularly watchful. Very early the next morning, he had awakened the landlord by shaking him roughly by the shoulder, and saying, " Here is the money for my night's lodging. If a man by the name of Green calls for me in a few days, give him that valise ; if not, here is an address to which you may send it. I am off. I suppose I hardly need tell you that your room is haunted. I lay with my back to the window; and in the bright space on the wall opposite, I kept seeing shadow-pictures like those they throw on a sheet from a magic-lantern ; only I had the same picture all night long, and that not a very agreeable one, — a man hanging from a gallows-tree. I concluded at last it might be a warning, and I mean to profit by it." The next day a man who gave his name as Detective Green did arrive, looking, as he said, for a burglar who had recently made away with a quantity of silver. He opened the black valise that had been left for him, and found every missing article.

How very unlike the different ghosts had been! — the white lady, the demon in the shape of a dragon, and the shadow of the gallows. And, not long after, an apparition was seen that was stranger still. The landlord hired a new hostler, a cruel boy, coarse and rough, with apparently no sensibilities to be troubled by spirits, and lodged him in the fated chamber. He woke the house with terrific yells, screaming that the ghost of a great yellow cat he had burned to death was coming to carry him off. The landlord felt that there was but a step from the sublime to the ridiculous, and that the boy had taken it. Cats could not have ghosts: that was too absurd. The thing must be explained. These stories and all the others that had been told, of clanking chains, creaking hinges to invisible doors, mysterious knockings, and other strange noises, must either be lies, or else there was some natural cause.

The next guests that came to his house were a

minister and his little daughter. The landlord told
them the history of the room. " It is the best I have
in the house," he said; " but I am afraid to give it to
this young lady, lest she should see something that
would frighten her. It is a pity, too; for just across the
hall is another large room which would do very nicely
for you, sir."

" Let me sleep there, papa," pleaded the little girl.
" If there are ghosts, I do not think that any of them
will harm me. All these people seem to have been
frightened by something wrong they had done. I
wonder what I shall see."

The night passed without alarm of any kind. When
the landlord served their breakfast, he could not restrain
his curiosity, and asked the little girl what she had seen.
" Nothing strange," said she. " I woke up once, and
saw the moon shining on a white figure gently swaying
back and forward before the window. I thought at first
it was an angel; but when I got out of bed, and went to
the window, I saw it was only the sign of the inn, — the
white wooden lion that hangs in front of the house."

On examination, it seemed most probable that this
was all that the others had seen. The noises were occa-

sioned by the creaking of its rusty hinges; and guilty imaginations had created from this simple object all the varied visions that had been seen in the room. The story became known: other people were found brave and innocent enough to sleep there. No more ghosts were seen; and the White Lion is now as prosperous an inn as you can find in any village in England. The Sunday after the little girl and her father stopped there, he preached a sermon from the text, " Conscience is a terror to the wicked, but a comfort to good men."

WHAT an old-fashioned,
clumsy, rusty pair of
scales they were! And
how many queer things
were weighed upon them
in that dingy little country store!

If they could have talked, they
might have told you the likings
of every family in the village; for
they were in the habit of giving
people just what they called for.
And the weights were so familiar
with the duty expected of them, that each prepared
to skip into the scales when his particular customer
entered the door, — from the brass thimble that clicked
impatiently to weigh out Miss Tibb's cent's worth of
snuff, to the great hollow projectile that Cousin Jack
sent home from the war, and was used for the heavier
commodities, such as flour, sugar, shot, and nails. The
set of weights had been complete once; but they had

gradually been lost in the course of years, Dr. Stockstill
having carried off the largest one to fasten to his horse's
hitching-strap, and Aunt Snip taken the big flat one
to keep the pork under the brine. Tommy Billings had
stolen the cunningest one of all to make a sinker for his
fish-line ; and so by degrees the regular weights had
been replaced by rather queer equivalents. Hepsy
knew them all by heart ; for she had helped her grandfather keep store ever since she was a very little girl.
When she began going to school, and the teacher
assigned her the tables of apothecary's and avoirdupois
weight for an arithmetic lesson, she glanced at the
title with a contemptuous " Guess I ought to know
that ; " and, when the class recited, astonished her
teacher by the glib announcement that —

4 brass thimbles make . . . 1 big pewter button.
5 of grandfather's pewter buttons make 1 glass door-knob.
6 glass door-knobs make . . the little flat-iron.
The little flat-iron, and 2 glass door-
knobs, and the brass extinguisher,
make . . . . 1 pound.
The big white stone, and a stove-lid,
make . . . . . . 10 pounds.
Cousin Jack's bombshell is . . 20 pounds.

Hepsy kept the two brass plates that belonged to the scales so well scoured that they shone like Ossian's shield. They were magic mirrors, which reflected the codfish or beeswax, horse-powders or tobacco, laid within them, and told by the alternating quantities of yarn and dye-stuff, or quinine and liver-pills, that went down to Aunt Tirzah's, whether the family were afflicted with the chills, or in good working condition ; told, too, something of the moral condition of the community, as the quantity of opium for old Deacon Feeblemind lessened, and the rate of tea, butter, eggs, spice, sugar, and soap for the family, with maple-sugar and hoarhound for the youngsters, increased. And they could have told how lazy Lem's weekly expenditure in spruce-gum and gin-ger-pop ceased, and he invested instead in garden-seeds after his father gave him that half-acre of meadow to cultivate for his very own. They could have told something of the love-affairs of half the academy girls : for Hepsy's grandfather kept the post-office ; and those great yellow business-envelopes that came regularly every week, and oftener, were frequently so bulky as to need extra postage, and were thrown into the scales for the brass thimbles to tell how many more stamps were required. Not only did the scales tell of the health, the morals, the wealth, and the love, of the community: they had their influence also in the intellectual world; for Miss Squibbs's MS. was duly weighed in them before being sent to the editor of "The Enlightener;" while the parson, who was caught at the store during a thunder-storm, was observed to gaze attentively and abstractedly at them during his entire stay; and his next sabbath's sermon, the best of the whole year, was from the text, "Thou art weighed in the balance, and found wanting." Babies were often brought in triumph, and laid upon the shining trays. Hepsy had herself been weighed here, she could not exactly remember when; but grandfather said she was the least of the lot, and only weighed seven and a half pounds. When Jack's bombshell came home from the war, it was hollow and empty; and as it happened to come on one of the anniversaries of Hepsy's birthday, and happened, on investigation, to contain just seven and a half pounds of shot, grandfather filled and plugged the aperture in order, as he said, "that in future years she might know to a bullet just how little she amounted to when she first came on the stage, and that it might take all pride and vain conceit out of her."

It would have been hard to find a girl with less pride than Hepsy. She was so gentle, so good-humored, and so serviceable, that her grandfather used often to say that she was worth her weight in gold. But even this compliment did not spoil her. " He would never have said so, you know," she thought, " if I had not weighed so little when I was a baby."

As the years went by, Hepsy went to the academy, and only tended store out of school-hours. Before she finished her course, her grandfather died, and a stranger bought the shop and its contents, all but the scales : these the old gentleman left in his will to Hepsy, with his blessing. The two bequests were inseparable : if she ever gave up the scales, the blessing would go too. The scales lay in a box, with the weights, up in the attic : for, since the stranger had taken possession of the store, Hepsy had given up her clerkship, and devoted her entire attention to her studies. Her grandfather had been something of an apothecary. She had liked best to see him weigh out and compound drugs ; and she had often wept foolish little tears because she was not a boy, and could not be a doctor.

It was examination week at the academy. Hepsy's class was to graduate. The programmes were out, and she saw her name in print for the first time, — Hephzibah Smith. No one had called her Hephzibah but grandfather, and he always added the signification of the name, " My delight is in her," and said that if ever a child was rightly called, Hepsy was; so that the name was a very sweet and precious one to her. The examination was looked forward to with more than ordinary interest by the graduating class this year. For Mr. DeClercq, the great man of the place, had been appointed to a foreign consulship, and was intending to sail for Europe soon after, with his family. He had been one of the school committee-men, and he knew well each member of Hepsy's class, and had announced, as soon as he received his appointment, that he would offer the position of governess for his children to the young lady graduating at the head of the class. This news had created intense rivalry among the girls; they were nearly all poor and ambitious. To go to Europe, to go to Europe! It seemed the most delectable thing that life could offer; and none coveted the opportunity more than Hepsy.

She had been so wholly absorbed in her studies, that not until a week before the eventful day had she given a thought to what she should wear on the occasion. But when she heard the other girls telling of their new dresses, sashes, and gloves, she awoke to the humiliating consciousness that she had only her old white dimity, without an extra scrap to make an overskirt, and so scant in the skirt that it would not admit of the wearing of a bustle. Hepsy went home sad at heart. She saw from a distance that the upright brooms of the tin-peddler, set like banners in his flaming red cart, had paused before her home; and she hastened her steps to tell him that it would be of no use to knock, for her mother did not need any thing in his line. "Perhaps not, miss," replied the peddler with engaging cheerfulness. "I should not wonder if my present stock would be more likely to suit you than your ma. You see I knew it was about commencement time; and I laid in a choice stock of millinery and dry goods, the newest and most fashionable styles."

Caleb Cox was gifted with a persuasive tongue; and,

before Hepsy knew, she had asked him into the house, and was looking at the tempting fabrics. There was a black-and-white summer silk which pleased her especially; a Boston lady had worn one quite similar at church several Sundays before, and Hepsy had studied it all through the service, and felt sure that she could make it up in the same style. Her mother was a good fitter; and by sewing steadily there was still time to have it done. It would make such a handsome suit for graduation, and, if she *should* go to Europe, she ought to have *one* stylish costume at least. "But, Hepsy," whispered her mother, "twenty dollars! And we haven't but fifteen between us."

"I don't mind having all in cash," said the obliging peddler. "I had just as lief, now, take out five dollars' worth in dicker, — soap-grease, rags, fresh-laid eggs, old iron and brass."

"Hepsy, bring the rag-bag," said Mrs. Smith. "I was thinking of making a new rag-carpet for the sitting-room; but, if there's enough to make out your dress, we'll let it go."

"I'll allow you three dollars for them rags," said the peddler.

"Couldn't you let us have the dress for that and fifteen dollars in cash?" asked Hepsy.

"No, I really don't believe I could. Twenty is the lowest figure I could let that pattern go at; and even then I oughtn't to take any thing but money in hand for it. Haven't you got any old brass andirons or knockers, or pewter platters?"

"Hepsy," said Mrs. Smith, "there are your scales."

"But I couldn't sell grandfather's legacy, you know."

"Great lumbersome things, — you had better bring them down: perhaps Mr. Cox won't want 'em any way." But Mr. Cox looked at them condescendingly, and concluded to accept them, with the weights, in lieu of the missing two dollars; and the sale was effected.

Examination-day came; the dress was finished, and Hepsy knew that for once she looked well. The first recitation was in chemistry; this was her strong point, and Hepsy led her classmates so markedly that the fact could not escape the notice of any present. Mr. DeClercq jotted her name down, and determined to pay particular attention to her replies throughout the day. Another old gentleman — a doctor from Boston — seemed much interested, and catechised her quite

95

severely on antidotes for poisons. Hepsy stood the test to his satisfaction; and he walked quite across the platform to inquire her name. The examination went on with varying results; but, at its close, the palm was awarded with justice to Cora Sturtevant. Hepsy crowded back her tears until she reached home. "It need not have been so," she said, "if I had only spent my time preparing for examination, instead of making my dress. To think, too, that to get it I gave up dear grandpa's scales! He said that I 'would lose a blessing' if I ever parted with them: and he was right; for the dress has lost me my trip to Europe. I wanted to go *so* much! and I never, never can have another opportunity. Oh, you wretched dress, I should like to tear you to atoms!"

"Hush, Hepsy!" said her mother, entering her room. "There is a strange gentleman down stairs, who wishes to speak with you."

It was the physician whom she had seen at the examination. "I have a proposition to make to you, Miss Smith," he began quite abruptly, "which may, however, seem somewhat beneath the notice of a young lady who has an opportunity of going abroad.

It is simply this: There is a vacancy among the nurses in the Massachusetts Woman's Hospital; we wish to fill it with a young woman who has some taste for the medical profession. If you should see fit to accept this position, you will acquire an excellent preparation for a medical course, and some practical knowledge of the treatment of certain cases, which will be invaluable to a young practitioner."

"But, sir," stammered Hepsy, "you did not stay through the examination; and I did not stand first in any of the other studies."

"So much the better: then you will not be embarrassed by a choice between two offers; and your mother gives me hope that you will accept mine."

"I have always wanted to be a physician," said Hepsy; "and if this is a stepping-stone to it"—

So, for a year, Hepsy served in the hospital, doing good to others while she was gaining valuable knowledge for herself. Many a sufferer echoed her grandfather's assertion that she was rightly named, and that their delight too was in her. At the close of the year the doctor said, "We hate to give you up, for you are worth your weight in gold; but, if you are going to the Medical College at Philadelphia, you ought not to stay with us any longer."

"I may come back again in the fall, doctor," replied Hepsy; "for, though I may be worth my weight in gold, I cannot reduce any of my possessions to hard cash; and Philadelphia looks a great way off."

While Hepsy was at home that summer, Caleb Cox, the peddler, called again; and she thought of the silk dress that had only been worn once, and had lost her the opportunity of a trip to Europe. She did not mind that now; for she had learned how much better it was to help herself, than to be helped, and how the very best thing of all was to help others. But there was one thing which she *did* mind. If she only had not parted with grandfather's scales, it seemed to her that she could have borne all the rest; but they were gone, and, worst of all, the blessing with them. A wild idea came to her; and she stopped Caleb Cox just as he was driving away. "Do you remember what you ever did with the scales and weights I gave you in part payment for a silk dress last year?"

"Wall, yaas," said Caleb. "My wife uses the brass plates to cook flapjacks on; and the other things I sent down with a lot of truck to the foundery, except the big bum-shell. I didn't durst drive so far with it a-rattling around amongst the old iron in my cart: was afeard there might be something explosive left in it. Mrs. Cox was fur busting it open to find out; but says I to her, ' Unless you want me to marry again before the summer's out, you let that alone. There was a woman down to Pot's Corners tried to open a nitro-glycerine can with a ax, and '— Wall, my wife concluded to let it be."

"Then you have got the bomb-shell yet," said Hepsy eagerly. "Oh, if you would just change it and the brass plates back again for the silk dress! it has only been worn once, and perhaps it will fit Mrs. Cox, or you could sell it to some one else."

Mr. Cox examined the dress, declared himself "willing to oblige," and the next day the brass plates and Cousin Jack's shell were again in Hepsy's possession. She ran up stairs hugging both in her arms in high glee; but, just as she gained the top, the heavy projectile slipped from her arms, and rolled bumpety-bump down the stairs again. Caleb Cox heard the noise, saw it coming, and, fearing to partake in the explosion which he was sure

787172 A

would follow, drove away from the door at the top of his horse's speed.

Hepsy hurried down stairs again, and found that the wooden stopper, which grandfather had fastened in so many years before, had become loosened by the fall, and had come out. The contents of the bomb were spilled all along the lower stairs and in the hall. They were not the explosives which Caleb Cox had feared, nor the leaden shot with which grandfather had first filled it, but gold dollars, shining gold dollars, that lay in a drift at her feet, and which grandfather had slipped into the shell one by one as he earned them, until there were seven pounds and a half of them, and Hepsy was really "worth her weight in gold."

"Who would have thought it!" exclaimed Mrs. Smith in indignation; "but father always had just that pernickety way of doing things."

And so Hepsy went to Philadelphia; she graduated with honor there, and is now pursuing her medical studies still further in Paris. The two brass plates have been cut down, and now form a part of a very dainty pair of apothecary's scales, with tiny gilded and silvered weights. Dr. Hephzibah Smith will use them some day in her office. Everybody says she is cut out for an old maid and a doctor; but Hepsy cannot help that, and does not care, for she was born under the constellations of the Virgin and the Scales.

PEEP THE SECOND.

ECLIPSES.

{ A RIDE WITH THE SUN }

THE sun was shining broadly outside of Joy's window, but she was still in her little lace-canopied bed. She was not asleep: she lay watching a broad sheet of rainbow-colored dancing motes that the sun was sifting through a crack in the shutter. They were finer than the flakes of flour that Dinah sent dusting through the sieve when she took it into her head to make bride's-cake, and of such beautiful colors that Joy's head fairly ached when she tried to think what a cake made from them would look like. She closed her eyes, not to see them any more, and listened. Grandma was singing. Grandma was a sweet, funny old lady, and she had a sweet but very funny voice. She had been a famous singer in her day,

had sung in the choir, and could carry her part triumph-
antly through the most intricate of the old fugue tunes;
but her sweet, old-fashioned voice was cracked, and had
all sorts of queer little quavers and quirks and unex-
pected trills and tremors in it; and her memory played
her as false as her voice, for she could not give the
words of the most familiar hymn correctly from beginning to end, but invariably mixed it with some other
with which it was connected in her mind from a similar-
ity of subject. She was singing now in a brisk, inspir-
ing way that ought to have roused Joy to instant
action, —

"Come, let us anew our journey pursue.
His adorable will let us gladly fulfil,
Roll round with the sun, and never stand still.
The rising sun that swift
Pursues his shining way,
And wide proclaims his Maker's praise
With every brightening ray.
The source of light, who bids the sun
On his burning axles run,
Stars like dust around him fly,
Strew the area of the sky.
And never stand still, and never stand still,
While they gladly fulfil his adorable will."

And then Joy knew by the brisk snapping that ensued, and by the commotion in the slanting wall of motes (for Joy when awake could never keep her eyes closed long), that grandma was beating the dust out of her rugs on the wrought-iron balustrade of the window next her own.

"I wonder how the man who wrote that hymn knew it," thought Joy. "But it was like that, just. The stars flew away on all sides, from the wheels of the Sun's chariot, like puffs of dust, and glittered like powdered gems as we whirled through them."

Joy had been to the sky-garden again. This time she had not strolled about with Puck; but old Sol himself, the glorious sun king, had taken her up into his golden car, and they had driven once around the many thousand mile track on which he exercises his fast trotters every day. Joy had been once to Jerome Park, and had seen a great many handsome turnouts. She had thought then that it must be very grand to sit beside the driver of a four-in-hand; but the sun drove a *twenty*-four-in-hand, for his steeds were the hours. Eight of them were white, eight black as night, and eight as gray and spectral as the pale horse in the

Revelation, or the sunless, shadowless skies of some twilights and dawns that she had known. She was quite certain that, with all the wealth and display at Jerome Park, there was not a team there that could compare with old Sol's. Joy had gone to sleep the night before with a heavy disappointment on her mind; and it was very kind and considerate in the Sun to come for her just at this time. She had tried so hard to make her table the most attractive one at the fair, and had hoped to hand in more money than any of the other girls, when Helen Earlewinne had stepped in, and gathered all her laurels. As Mrs. Fairchild said, Joy had been completely eclipsed. She had said too, that it would be a good lesson for her little girl; that Joy was growing too fond of approbation, and too confident of her own powers: a little taking down would be good for her. But Joy's mother was wrong here: the child's heart was swelling with the injustice of the thing; and mortified pride, disappointed ambition, and a spice of revenge, were making a true witches' caldron of her breast. This was how it all happened. A fair had just taken place for the benefit of the orphanless children, as Bobby called the little folks who lived in the great un-homelike brick building that people called the Home. It was a children's fair, all the departments being assigned to children, while the grown-up ladies had nothing but the general management. Joy had the art-table. It was just the one that she coveted most; and she had worked hard for two months to make it a success. She had made two handsome chromo scrap-books; had been around to all the book-stores, and obtained, at low prices, engravings, stereoscopic views and other photographs, with the privilege of returning those unsold; she had a few very pretty brackets and photograph-frames in Sorrento carving of holly and ebony. But what she was especially proud of was her decorated china. Joy belonged to Miss Earle's paint-ing-class; and she had interested all of the girls, some of whom painted very nicely, in her table. Together they purchased a number of plain Parian vases of grace-ful shape, and a quantity of terra-cotta flower-pots and hanging-baskets; these they decorated very prettily with flowers and vines, arabesques and silhouettes from Paul Konewka. The things were beauties, and could not fail to be one of the features of the fair. Miss Earle herself had contributed a beautiful painting on porce-

lain, of arbutus and ferny moss. Besides all this, Uncle
Briar had given Joy ten dollars, not for the fair, but for
her very own ; though he consented to her request to
be allowed to purchase something from her own table
with it as a souvenir of the fair, and to help swell
the sum which she hoped to hand to the committee ;
and Joy had set her heart on Miss Earle's arbutus.
Just at the last moment, Helen Earlewinne had appeared, and said that she had several boxes of fine
French flowers which she had learned to make when at
school in Paris ; and, if Joy would give her a corner
of her table, she would sell them for the benefit of the
fair. Of course, Joy could not refuse. But, when they
arranged the table, Helen caught sight of the vases and
flower-pots, and exclaimed at once, " Oh, how fortunate !
these are just what I want to mount my flowers in.
You will see how lovely they will look." And in half an
hour, Helen had fulfilled her promise ; for each vase
contained a dainty little bouquet of rosebuds, heliotrope,
and fuchsia, or carnation pinks, vivid geraniums, and
snowy lily-of-the-valley, so natural that it needed the
sense of touch to detect the deception, while from the
flower-pots there rose hyacinths exquisitely imitated

from nature, and rose-bushes whose every thorn and leaf were copied from June's own handiwork. From the hanging-baskets trailed waxy-leaved ivies or other vines; and in the centre of each stood a mottled begonia or other foliage-plant. The flowers thus arranged took up more than half the table, so that it was Joy who had the "corner." Late in the afternoon, and just before all was ready, a man appeared, carrying a statuette of Mercury, in plaster. "I bought this for you at Casters & Chizzler's," said Helen: "they only asked twelve dollars for it, as it was for the fair, and we can sell it in shares. At fifty cents a chance, we shall only have to sell twenty-four to pay for it; and after that, all will be clear gain."

"But," said Joy, "I don't think that raffling is right. I know they are going to do it at all the other tables, but I didn't mean to have any thing of the kind at mine."

"I don't see that you can do any thing else now," said Helen, "for I bought it in your name. I was sure you would jump at the chance, and I don't believe we could find any one to buy such an expensive thing outright. Now, you needn't look so cross; there isn't a bit of risk, for one of my gentlemen friends has promised to take all the shares that are unsold at the close of the evening."

Helen was several years older than Joy, and she had usurped the lead so naturally that there seemed nothing for Joy to do but to yield the point. "Very well," she said reluctantly, "if you will sell the shares, and take the whole responsibility"—

"Certainly," said Helen, eagerly placing the statuette in the centre of her flowers; "and see what a handsome ornament it makes for your table." The gleaming white figure certainly had a very fine effect supported on all sides by masses of brilliant flowers; and Joy could not help feeling that it made her poor little chromos and photographs look very insignificant and mean by comparison.

The flowers, or the pots and vases which held them, proved very popular, and sold rapidly; but when the evening was nearly over Helen came to Joy with a long face, saying that she had only sold four shares for her Mercury. "That is too bad," said Joy; "but I don't see that it makes a great deal of difference if your friend is willing to take all the rest."

"He said he would yesterday," said Helen; "but to-night I can only get him to take four shares."

Joy ceased looking after the interests of her own articles, and devoted herself to offering the Mercury shares to all who stopped at her table. She met with no success, however, for every one seemed to have done spending money for that evening. Then Joy in desperation bought the remaining twenty shares with the ten-dollar bill that Uncle Briar had given her, with the sinking feeling at her heart that after all not a cent of it would go to the fair, but all would belong to the firm that had furnished the statuette. "Of course I shall draw it," she thought; "and then I will give it back to the fair, and they can sell it at auction with the other things left over." But the strange fate that presides over lotteries decreed that Helen's friend should hold the lucky number that drew the Mercury, which he immediately presented to her. Three dollars was the highest sum that had been offered for Miss Earle's water-color, and Joy could have cried when she saw it carried away; the photographs were all sold at only an advance of a few cents over their original price; the chromo scrap-books would not sell at all, and were disposed of at the auction for about half their cost. When the reports were handed in, Helen Earlewinne gave thirty dollars as her share, while Joy could only show four dollars and thirty-seven cents. "I am afraid the art table would not have amounted to much without Miss Helen's assistance," was the remark made by the president of the fair; and poor Joy ran and hid in the coal-closet, where she could cry without being seen.

Yes, Joy had been completely eclipsed, but it did not seem likely to do her good. She had been humble enough before: she was humiliated now; and such an experience is seldom a beneficial one. Her mother's words made an impression on her mind, but she did not quite understand it. "Father, what is an eclipse?" she asked, as they rode home through the night.

Mr. Fairchild began a scientific description and explanation of the phenomenon, just such a one as he would have given to the junior class at the university, but illustrated it from the present surroundings by calling the axle of the front wheel of the carriage the earth, the lantern the sun, and a cake of mud that had adhered to the tire of the wheel, and was revolving rapidly around the axle-earth, the moon. The only trouble was that the revolutions of the mud moon were so swift that it made Joy nearly dizzy to keep it in view; and her father's demonstration, with its learned allusions to parallax, the sun's photosphere, heliocentric longitude, and the perturbation of the elliptic motion of the moon, was quite as difficult to follow. When she tried to apply it to her own case, and see just how it was that she had been eclipsed, the problem became still more complicated; and she became hopelessly puzzled in trying to decide whether Helen Earlewinne had come into conjunction with the carriage lantern, or whether the daub of mud in its perturbations had occasioned an obscuration of her decorated pottery. Mr. Fairchild, in a pause in his lecture, saw by the dreamy look in his little girl's eyes, and the yawn suppressed behind the polite little hand, that she had not understood a word of his explanation. "It is too hard for you, is it not, Joy?" he said kindly. "Well, all that you need try to understand is, that one body is eclipsed when another throws it completely into the shade."

That was simple enough certainly, but it did not make her feel any happier; and she went to sleep with very unkind thoughts toward Helen Earlewinne, who had so completely thrown her in the shade. Scarcely had her eyelids closed, when the great, genial Sun reined in his twenty-four-in-hand at her window, and invited her to take a ride. Joy clambered up by his side, and was delighted to find that from her elevated seat she could look away across the sky-garden, and see not only the part she had visited with Puck, but vaster unexplored regions stretching away on every side. She wondered if it was all as beautiful as the portion with which she was already familiar. She could see a silvery white river gliding placidly through the heavenly fields. It was so calm, and the country through which it flowed so level, that it made her think of some views she had seen of Holland, especially as here and there she caught sight of tall mills not very unlike the windmills that dotted the pictures she had seen of that country.

"What river is that?" she asked of the Sun.

"It is the Milky Way," replied her escort. "We shall have a better view of it after we pass the judge's stand;" and the Sun reached far forward, and touched his leader's ear lightly with the tassel of his whip, making his team fairly spin around the magnificent race-course.

What a beautiful, broad, gently curving river it was!

Little elves were rowing about upon it in butter boats, some of which were piled with great rolls of butter like rafts of logs. These boats seemed to have just left some one or other of the mills; and Joy suddenly noticed that these tall towers were shaped exactly like churns, and some of them had streaming from the high flagstaff that surmounted them a pennon with the inscription, " Buttermilk Mills." The frothing cascade which poured down the race at their sides was certainly real buttermilk; and the mill-wheels were not arranged on the ordinary plan, but looked more like the dashers of churns than any thing else. There was a pleasant, busy, splashing sound going on inside; and the elves with butter-paddles and butter-knives for oars kept busily coming and going.

A little farther down, the banks of the river were formed of cliffs of milk-toast, whose strata the elves were separating by means of toasting-forks and gravy-spoons. The great slabs had been so coated with the washings of the river, that they were as white and smooth as marble; while, between the crevices, streams had oozed and trickled, leaving long white stalactites on the rough brown edges.

Beyond Milk Toast Quarries, the river was yellow with things which Joy at first fancied were water-lilies, but which were in reality custard-flowers. Then its *curd*ling waves swept round Cream Cheese Castle, a massive round structure, and next they darted in a torrent of foam down Whipped Cream Cascade. After this, the Milky Way seemed to flow through a colder climate; for it was frozen, and little men and women were skating upon it. Some, more industrious than the others, were sawing and cutting the ice into fanciful shapes, — great shafts like Bunker Hill Monument, and fluted columns, buff, chocolate, and rosy-tinted. Joy was not surprised to see that these columns were variously labelled Vanilla, Lemon, and Strawberry; for, as cream always rises to the surface of milk, of course the ice formed on the Milky Way would be icecream. Neither was it at all astonishing that, after the ice was removed, the river should flow on with pale blue waves, and be called Skim Milk Canal. She did not care to follow its meanderings any farther, especially as the Sun told her that it next moved sluggishly through Sour Milk Marsh; and she turned her gaze from the landscape, and fixed it upon her companion;

and, as she did so, was surprised to find that though he had a shining countenance, she could yet look him squarely in the face without being dazzled as she had always been when attempting the same experiment from the earth. The Sun seemed to read her thoughts; for he answered just as though she had spoken, —

"That is because you have never really seen my face: what you have seen is only my golden shield that hangs here by the side of my chariot."

"Cousin Myrtle looks at it every day," said Joy, "through the coast-survey" (the coast-survey was the name of one of her father's telescopes). "She is keeping a diary of the sun-spots for Uncle Briar: she paints a little picture of them every day, and dates it, so that she knows just how they change. Uncle Briar is going to have them all printed in color for a book he is writing."

"And what do you suppose the sun-spots are?" asked the Sun.

"When I thought it was your face," replied Joy, "I thought they were freckles: it's the sun that makes them come on *our* faces, and I should think *you* would have lots of them. But, now that they are on your shield, I don't know what they are, unless the wheels of your carriage going round have splashed mud on it, as the perturbation of the moon did on our carriage."

"Nonsense," said the Sun with a laugh: "they are scars and dints that I have received in my battles with the Powers of Darkness. I am a great warrior; never a day passes but I shiver countless lances of light against the shadow demons in your world. But I don't suppose you know any thing about fighting: you are only a little girl."

"I have read about Arthur's Table Round," said Joy modestly, — "King Arthur's, who went out through all the world to help the weak and the oppressed, and to fight with every kind of wrong."

"So do I," said the Sun. "Each twenty-four hours I make a pilgrimage all around your earth, kissing the tears out of the eyes of the violets, helping every aspiring plant to climb up a little higher than it was the day before, and making every evil and shameful thing fly before me and hide itself, as the snakes do, in dark dens. I have a great deal of work to do, and a great many battles to fight in your world, little girl, but I don't mean to tell you of them: if you are thoughtful and observant, you will find them out for yourself; and, if you should not happen to find them out, I don't know that it makes much difference after all. I am like Arthur's knights in one thing at least: —

> " ' My good blade carves the casques of men,
>   My tough lance thrusteth sure,
>   My strength is as the strength of ten,
>   Because my heart is pure. ' "

Joy looked at the great Sun in admiration; what a worker he was, to be sure! He was busier every day and always than she had been the past two months for the fair; and yet no one took any notice of what he did, in the way of giving him the credit for it. She had never heard any one say, " How very kind it is of the Sun to dry up all that mud, so that we can go to the picnic to-day!" or, " Don't you think it was very thoughtful in the Sun not to forget to rise this morning? " They did not even, when Christmas came, get him up a present and a vote of thanks, as they did for the postman, who " must find it so tiresome to keep going the same rounds every morning." And, worst of all, her father had told her that every little while the Sun was totally eclipsed, just as she had been; and nobody was sorry for him.

"Poor Sun!" said Joy, the tears filling her eyes, "*I* am sorry for you. I have been eclipsed, and I know what it is like."

"Pooh! that's nothing," replied the Sun, who seemed to have followed her entire train of thought. "You may think you know what it is to be eclipsed; but I don't believe you really do, if you think it is any thing to cry about."

"Father said being eclipsed was being thrown into the shade," said Joy.

"Now, I call that a very poor definition," replied the Sun. "When I am eclipsed I am never thrown into the shade: I am just as bright-faced and warm-hearted as I was before. What do you suppose I care, if a few people down in your little world lose sight of me for a few minutes? It brings the Moon into notice, and pleases her, you know; and I like to please the Moon, for she never did me any harm, or meant any malice in simply coming between me and the public."

The Sun's words started a new train of thought in

Joy's mind. Why shouldn't she, too, be as bright-faced and warm-hearted as ever, in spite of *her* eclipse? Perhaps Helen Earlewinne had not meant to do her an injury by her own success; and, after all, she could not help carrying off the honors of the day any more than the moon could.

"Then, you know," continued the Sun, "that I am never totally eclipsed except to a very small portion of the world at the same time. While just in one particular line it is just the same to people as if I had gone out of the heavens, to the rest of the world I am of as much consequence as I ever was."

Was not that true of her too? To be sure, the committee ladies thought that Joy might have been quite as well omitted from the workers for the fair; but her father and mother, and Cousin Myrtle and Uncle Briar, and Miss Earle's girls, and Helen Earlewinne herself, knew how much she had helped.

"And there is little Mercury," said the Sun: "no one thinks how instrumental I am in their getting a peep at him. Astronomers last year were all aching to see him; but they couldn't have done it, if I had not been eclipsed."

Joy did not see, just then, how this point was applicable to her, though she did a little later in the night. Evidently some one wanted the statuette of Mercury which she had helped purchase. She wondered who it was.

"So, you see," said the Sun, "I think your father's definition of an eclipse unworthy of his reputation as an astronomer. I should like to know what the scientific world in general would think of such a slipshod use of terms."

"Oh! papa did give me a very scientific explanation of it all," said Joy eagerly, anxious to defend her father to the irate old Sun, who was fast growing hot with indignation. "It was so very scientific, and had so much about parallax and axles and the daub of mud that kept going round and round, that I could not understand it at all; but that wasn't my papa's fault."

"I don't see why he said any thing about parallax," grumbled the Sun, "though that matter is easy enough to understand. Didn't he try to tell you what it was?"

"He said," replied Joy, speaking very slowly and distinctly, for she wished to be sure of giving her father's exact words, — "he said that parallax was the change of place which an object undergoes when viewed from two different stations."

"Certainly, certainly," assented the Sun. "Now, if you were walking under an apple-tree, the apples could look down upon you; but if you were sailing over it in a balloon, you could look down upon the apples: that would be a case in which the parallax would amount to 180°. Did you never notice how very different things look when viewed from different standpoints? This question of parallax will keep coming up all your life long, and you might as well try to understand it now. People make enormous mistakes in their life-problems by not allowing for it: they think, because a thing seems to them to occupy a certain position, it really *is* there, and never take into consideration the fact that if they changed their place of observation the object in question might appear to be in a different place too. Now don't yawn, for I am going to tell you why I have been talking to you about parallax. I presume you think Helen Earlewinne just about the unkindest girl in the world; now, don't you?"

"No-o-o," said Joy.

"Well, you did last evening; and what you ought to

do now, is what the astronomers always do before they finish calculating an eclipse, — make the *correction for parallax.* You should try to see Helen Earlewinne from some other standpoint."

" I should like to," said Joy submissively, "but I don't see how I can. You see, she is such a great girl, we are not in the same set at all."

"Would you like to look into her room at this very moment?" asked the Sun.

" If it would make me like her any better."

" Answered like a true-hearted little girl. I cannot go with you, for she would be surprised and frightened to see me at this time of night; but I will set you on the back of my black leader there, and, as you pass Helen's window, you can look in: she will not see you, for his flowing mane will cover you all over like a mantle."

The Sun dismounted from his chariot, and, walking along beside his handsome tandem team, lifted Joy to a seat on the very blackest of his horses. It was named Midnight, and had a white star in its forehead. Then the Sun vanished, and Joy knew that she was looking into Helen's room. It was simply furnished; for, though

126

the Earlewinnes had been wealthy, they were now in straitened circumstances. Helen was speaking to her mother. She seemed to have been relating the experiences of the evening; for the first words that Joy heard were, —

"And so, mother, all of my flowers were sold,—all of them. I don't regret the work I put into them. But I don't believe they would have gone, if the little mistress of the art-table had not let me have some of the prettiest pots and vases to put them in that you ever saw. She was the most unassuming little thing; she quite won my heart. I mean to know her better some day. And when that wretched Mr. Reed would not fulfil his promise about the statuette, she bought all the shares herself. I was so provoked when he drew it! And, to make the matter worse, he must needs present it to me. I was so mortified, I wanted to give it right to that little Joy Fairchild; but there was such a quiet dignity about the little thing, that actually I hadn't the face to do it. She said so simply, ' I did not want the Mercury; and all I am sorry for is, that the orphans will not be any better off for it.' Dear little thing! you've no idea, mother, how insignificant she made me feel. But the

127

orphans shall have some pleasure from it; for I am going to take that great bracket of mine, and make a back to it of the piece of green velvet that you gave me for my winter bonnet. It will throw out the statuette finely; and then I'll set it up in the schoolroom at ·the Home. It is the most dreary place you ever saw; and the little things are pining for something beautiful to look at. I wish they could know that they owed it to Joy Fairchild ; but since they can't, you may be sure that no one of them will ever hear of my name in connection with it."

" That was just like the sky-garden too," Joy thought, " for people thanked the Moon as little as they did the Sun for causing the eclipse, and letting them see Mercury." And how unconscious Helen Earlewinne was! she did not appear to know that she had eclipsed Joy at all. Joy felt her heart warm toward her more when she went on, " And, mother, I am so glad! I have found out what her favorite flower is, — arbutus. I can imitate it perfectly ; and I mean to make her a long trailing wreath of it to wear on her spring hat next season. I would rather she should know I sent it, on one account; for I should like to have her like me: but, I guess, on the whole, it will be nicer to send it to her in some way that will not be likely to betray me."

At this point, Joy was seized with such an irresistible desire to kiss Helen, that if her coal-black steed had not· borne her very swiftly on, she would have sprung through the window.

"What do you think of Helen Earlewinne now?" asked the Sun as he helped her to dismount.

"She is just sweet!" exclaimed Joy enthusiastically.

"Parallax! parallax!" he replied pleasantly; "and eclipses are not such bad things either. My gray horse, Dawn, is just over *your* window now. Perhaps you had best slide down, and some other time you shall have another ride."

And Joy lay in her bed. Was it all a dream? She thought so, until a package was left mysteriously at her door containing a garland of arbutus: then she knew that it was all true. Helen Earlewinne became her dearest friend; but she never told her of her ride, or of the unkind feelings she had had toward her before. But, as her mother wished, she had learned not to care very much whether people appreciated her efforts, but, whether they did or not, to work on just as earnestly.

John Brown's favorite couplet, that grandma sang so often, ran in her mind every time she looked at a sunrise; for she knew that the brave old Sun would watch her throughout the day, and be ashamed of any faint-heartedness on the part of his little friend; and so she too repeated the couplet after grandma, —

"Count that day lost whose low-descending sun
Views from thy hand no worthy action done."

PART II.

TALES OF THE ZODIAC.

SCORPIO

BOBBY'S COMPOSITION

CORPIO suggested no story to either Cousin Myrtle or Uncle Briar, and this sign of the zodiac might have been slighted if it had not been for the youngest member of the party.

"Never you mind, Cousin Myrtle," said Bobby Copernicus: "I've got a composition to write, and I'll write it on scorpiums. I always like to write about some kind of a beast. All you have to do is to go straight to Goldsmith's 'Animated Nature,' and read all he says about 'em, and then write down all he said that you can remember, and all you know about it your own self."

"But isn't that stealing?" asked Cousin Myrtle. "When authors do so, and print what they write, it is called plagiarism."

"Oh, mine ain't plaguey-ism," said Bobby proudly. "Father explained all that to me. He said when I took any thing out of a book, I must be very careful to mention my authority, tell just what book it was, and who wrote it, and then it was all right. I do that every time now; you'll see."

And so they did, on the following Saturday evening, when a small but appreciative audience listened with rapt attention to —

SCORPIUMS.

Scorpiums are a very big kind of bug. Mr. Goldsmith says in his "Animated Nature," that in Africa they grow as big as lobsters. But I guess that is a whopper, unless it was a very little baby lobster about as big as a fiddler. A fiddler is a kind of crab they have down to Newport. They call them fiddlers because one of their claws is shaped like a vialscentium, and the other like a trombone or a clarionet, or a kettle-drum, or something, I forget what it was Uncle Briar said. Any way, I couldn't see any difference in 'em. They looked just like claws, that was all. And I think Uncle Briar must see very queer out of his eyes sometimes.

For Cousin Myrtle has nice pumpkin-colored hair, and he told her it was woven sunshine, and sunshine is just *no* color, like water or glass. I asked mother about it, and she said that was just the way father used to talk before they was married, and that lovers saw every thing through rose-colored spectacles. But, if that is so, I should have thought he would have thought her hair was red. Lovers must be queer things, any way. Mr. Goldsmith says in his " Animated Nature " that they are the meanest things living, for they eat up their own relations quicker'n any thing. Oncet there was a man had one big one and thirty-seven little ones in a pickle-bottle, and it ate 'em every one up; and one little one clumb on to its mother's back so it couldn't eat it, and held on tight until it had eaten its mother, which I think just served her right. But father says it is very wrong to eat mothers.

Goldsmith says in his " Animated Nature," that they are a great deal more poisonous than tarantulas. Tarantulas are spiders. But in Texas they call whiskey tarantula juice, which I think is a very good name for it, for the temperance man told us at Sunday school that at the last it biteth like a serpent and stingeth like a yellow-jacket. Yellow-jacket is hornets. I never tasted any, but I should think it must be a good deal like Jamaica ginger. Whiskey causes more intemperance than any other kind of unhappiness in the world. That is what the man said we must always remember.

Goldsmith says in his " Animated Nature," that there are nine different varieties of this dangerous insect, distinguished by their colors, — ash color, rusty-iron color, green color, greenish-yellow color, yellowish-green color, yellow color, and seven others that I don't remember; of which one is more venomous than the other four.

Father says some boys remind him of scorpiums, specially of that little one that ate up his mother. He said there was a boy one Fourth of July that fired off all his fire-crackers under his mother's rocking-chair, what was real sick at the time. And he said that boy was as mean as the little scorpium. But he didn't say how that boy's father wolloped me for it, nor how the next Fourth of July he took the money my grandpa sent me for torpedoes, and bought me a microscope with it instead, because microscopes was more instructive. And then, mother wouldn't let me have no satisfaction out of it, but burnt up her needle-case chockfull of ants that I was saving to examine, and took me right up stairs, and shut me up in her closet. I think microscopes are humbugs. Goldsmith says in his "Animated Nature" that their mouths are principally composed of jaws, all notched into each other like a circular saw-mill. There was a little boy once that fell into one, and was tored up quicker than a wink. I know our teacher wishes sometimes that she was a circular saw-mill. For boys — I mean *some* boys — can be just as teasin' as any thing to school-teachers. Goldsmith says in his "Animated Nature," that he thinks their malignity and venomossity has been greatly exaggerated, for he knew a man that tried all he could to make one bite him, and it wouldn't. I saw one in a bottle oncet at the museum, or else it was a horned toad or a centipede, I don't remember which. And there were so many reptiles and other lizards in with it, that I don't remember exactly what it looked like. And this is all I know about scorpiums. A man named Mr. Goldsmith has written about them some too, in a book called "Goldsmith's Animated Nature." But it wouldn't pay you to read it, for he doesn't know much more about them than I do.

RANDMA had many curiosities in her room, and Joy loved dearly to look them over. To be allowed to do so, however, was a high privilege which was only granted at rare intervals, and was prized accordingly. On one of Grandma's especially gracious days, Joy was seated, with all the timidity of respectful anticipation, on the extreme edge of one of the high-backed May-flower chairs, while she examined the contents of a drawer in a quaintly carved red-cedar cabinet, Grandma's pet repository for her treasures. This particular drawer seemed to be devoted to Indian curiosities. There were jasper and carnelian arrow-heads, very rudely carved, from the battle-field of Bloody

Brook, where the old records of the family stated that a remote ancestor had been "slayne by yᵉ bloodthirsty salvages." There were the arrows that Cousin Dick, who died with Custer, had sent home the very summer of the massacre, — long light reeds fastened to the heavy heads with a wax so soft that the warmth of the body would cause it to melt, leaving the arrowhead in the wound when an attempt was made to withdraw the shaft; and others designed with an equally inhuman ingenuity, with spiral channels winding around the shaft like the grooves of a screw, leaving open passage-way for scarlet rivulets, which would soon allow the victim to bleed to death. There were a few arrowheads of ancient nations, brought from foreign countries by friends of Grandma's; but what most excited Joy's curiosity was a piece of a broken bow, of some polished expensive wood, the long bow-string, with a faded green silken tassel, being still attached to the unshattered end.

"Did you ever hear of a little winged boy," said Grandma, with a smile, "who is very skilful in archery practice, but has a very cruel habit of always aiming his arrows at human hearts? See, here is his portrait on the back of this miniature of my father."

"Do you mean Cupid, Grandma?" asked Joy. "There is another picture of him on the valentine Willie Softs sent me last spring. I don't see, though, how Cupid could have used such a large bow as this must have been before it was broken: the string is nearly five feet long."

"It is an English bow, my dear, such as English ladies of quality amused themselves with a hundred years ago. It came from England with several more like it, and witnessed many a fashionable merry-making given by the ladies of New York to the British officers, who then occupied the city."

"O Grandma!" exclaimed Joy enthusiastically, "it ought to go to the Centennial. Do tell us about it. Is it a love story? and were you in it?"

"Yes, and no," replied Grandma. "It acted an important part in an old romance; but you must think your grandmother a more ancient lady than she is, if you fancy that she could have figured in it. My mother lived in New York throughout the entire Revolution. Her father, Heinrich Van Vechten, did not take any active part on either side of that great conflict. But he was noted as being one of the most bountiful entertainers in the city, and his hospitable house overflowed now with Tory, and now with patriot guests. This created a very gay life for my mother, who was then a young lady. She formed the acquaintance of most of the prominent men of the day; and the leaders of both sides regarded the brilliant Josephine Van Vechten with equal admiration. Her home was situated on the bank of the Hudson, near the site of Columbia College, and was then considered quite out of town. She knew most of the professors and many of the older students. There were two, Alexander Hamilton and David Dalzell, who were frequent callers. They were both young men of talent, and stanch patriots; and from their stirring conversation, Josephine, who was at first as indifferent as her father to politics, became interested in the revolutionary movement.

"After the defeat of our army on Long Island, on the 27th of August, 1776, most of the men noted for their patriotic sympathies left the city; but young Dalzell remained, and, to Josephine's astonishment, mingled more unreservedly than was his wont in the social entertainments of the time. He was of good family, and was well received everywhere. Some of his relatives were Tories, and his own sentiments were not generally known. He was not as outspoken now as he had been in the old familiar talks the winter before, when he brought his orations to read to her before delivering them at the college; and Josephine wondered if he was changing, and felt her admiration for him subside a little. He seemed so very friendly with some of the young British officers, she could hardly reconcile it with his professed admiration for Washington, with whose acquaintance he had been honored but a short time previous. It was a sad disappointment to her to discover that one whom she had regarded as quite a hero was so false or fickle. She told him so one evening at a reception at Sir Henry Clinton's, when he reproached her with having changed, and no longer extending toward him the old friendly familiarity. 'Josephine,' he said, replying to her quick retort, 'you used to be a patriot too; and you cannot have seen me at more English entertainments than you have yourself attended; and I have never seen you look displeased on receiving attentions from Lord Percy or Count Knyphausen.'

"'I am only a girl,' she replied, while tears of vexation

started to her eyes; 'but, if I could serve my country by staying away, you may be sure I never would attend one of these gatherings.'

" 'Can you not imagine,' said young Dalzell mysteriously, 'that I have not changed at all; that in associating intimately with those in the confidence of the British commander, I may be able to serve my country better than by running away, or bringing suspicion upon myself by foolhardiness?'

"A glance of intelligence was exchanged between the two. She understood now; and, though a spy's calling was the most dangerous he could have chosen, her heart gave a little leap of triumph at the assurance that he was not recreant to his convictions. There was a little pause, and then she said cordially, —

" 'If I can help you in any way' —

" 'Thank you,' replied David Dalzell; 'but I fear that my own mission here is drawing to a close. There are a number of suspected characters about whom a red circle is being drawn; I think that I have so far succeeded in keeping out of it. But, once in that situation, I shall have to give up the game, and leave the city as quickly as possible.'

"'Perhaps,' said Josephine, 'I can enact Jonathan to your David. You know the old Scripture story, — how Jonathan discovered that mischief was devised against his friend, and warned him of it in his conversation, with the ingenious double meanings at the target-shooting by the stone Ezel, so that " only Jonathan and David knew the matter," while the lad who gathered up the arrows "knew not any thing." I will try to find out to-night whether your suspicions have any foundation, and will warn you if you are in danger.'

"'Your suggestion is a capital one; and there is no time to be lost. I have important business which will prevent my remaining here longer this evening; and I do not see how I can come out to your house to-morrow. Can you not manage to be in the city during the day?'

"'I am invited to the archery party at Sir Guy Carleton's in the afternoon.'

"'Then we can make a genuine Jonathan-and-David affair of it; for I will call there during the day, and. instead of leaving, manage to secrete myself in the boat-house at the foot of the garden. One of the targets is fastened against its side; and, when you are standing near it, I can easily hear all you say.'

"'Then remember,' said Josephine, 'what you said about the red line being drawn around the suspected ones, and about giving up the game; for I shall try to use those words in some way.'

"'I trust all to you,' replied David Dalzell as he took leave: 'you are my last, my only dependence.'

"'I pray I may not prove a broken reed for you to lean upon,' responded Josephine.

"For two hours longer, Josephine danced and chatted and flirted with different officers. Twice her mother came to remind her that it was time to leave; but she begged so earnestly for just a few minutes more that Mrs. Van Vechten yielded. No one had ever before seen Josephine so animated and apparently carried away with the pleasure of the evening. She had never been so witty, or so universally admired; and on no other occasion had she appeared to better advantage. To Josephine herself, the two hours seemed frightfully short. She never lost sight of her aim, and from each of her partners adroitly extracted an additional scrap of information, until she knew for a certainty that David Dalzell's fears were not groundless. He was more than suspected: it might even now be too late to save him.

"That night she hardly slept; and all the next morning she glided about the house in a fever of anxiety. What if he were already arrested! Executions followed with such terrible rapidity, that they might at this very moment be leading him out to be hung.

"At length the hour arrived for the archery party. For a wonder, Miss Van Vechten was very prompt, being among the earliest arrivals. A long garden and lawn stretched back of Sir Guy Carleton's residence to the river-side. At each extremity, large targets were erected. Beginning at the mansion, the party were to shoot at the one by the side of the boat-house until all their arrows were exhausted; and then, walking to that end of the field, collect their shafts, and aim at the other target. The *fête* was one that Josephine had looked forward to with high anticipation. She wore a costume prepared expressly for the occasion, of green flowered brocade, with a pointed hat of the same material, and a snow-white ostrich feather that curled over its great green hollow like the crest of a wave at Long Branch. But the mermaiden within the wave had any thing but a merry face. She was noted for the exactitude of her shots, and for her magnificent pose at the instant the arrow quitted the string. But this afternoon she was remarkably reckless. Not one of her arrows touched the golden centre, and not once did she strike her favorite Diana attitude, with the lithe hand and arm curved gracefully above the puffings on her shoulder. She was strangely silent too, until they took their second stand, by the river; and then several times her voice rose high above the rest in a way that was almost unladylike, and with a cutting intensity in its quality that no one had ever noticed before. The first time that she spoke was when young Col. Bartlett, who led her side, took his turn. 'You are inside the red circle!' The words had a sharp vibrant ring in them; and the colonel answered somewhat testily, 'Well, what if I am? that is not bad : red is next to gold.' He looked at her in surprise when she repeated the same exclamation in the same shrill tones after the shooting of the next two players. 'Why, Josephine Van Vechten!' exclaimed one of the girls, 'I think you must be getting near-sighted. That is my arrow in the green circle. It is your turn now; see if you can do any better.'

"Josephine took her stand, placing the end of her bow against her right foot in the scientific position for stringing it, but drawing the cord so smartly that it snapped at once. 'There is nothing to be done,' she cried in a tone of vexation, 'but to give up the game.'

"'Try my bow,' said one of her friends.

"'They are all alike,' she replied, 'all equally unreliable. This was my main dependence; and it can do nothing further for me.'

"Later, when they were talking of long shots, one of the company boasted that he could shoot across the river; and, on his attempting it, Josephine called to the darting arrow, 'Fly, fly! quick, quick! to the Jersey shore.'

"'That *would* be a long shot,' said Col. Bartlett with a laugh, and then he attempted to engage Josephine in conversation. But her replies were very low and brief; and no one recollected to have heard her speak aloud that afternoon, except in the odd exclamations which I have repeated.

"While the party was going on, a band of soldiers with a warrant of arrest were searching everywhere, without success, for David Dalzell. And a few days later, Sir

Guy Carleton told Josephine that his row-boat had been stolen in a mysterious manner that very evening.

"It was not till after peace was declared, that David Dalzell returned, and told how he drifted down the river, passed the sentries under cover of the midnight with muffled oars, and reached the American camp the next day in safety.

"Theirs was a stately, old-fashioned wedding. The artist who painted the miniature on ivory, which was to be David's wedding-gift to his wife, was not surprised that he wanted a picture of Cupid, with bow and arrows, on the reverse. Young men often had such romantic notions. But he could not conceive why my father should insist that the bow should be represented as broken."

CAPRICORNUS

THE TURKISH RUG.

AND blue and purple and scarlet and fine linen and goat's hair, and rams' skins dyed red, and badgers' skins," said Joy softly to herself, as Cousin Myrtle passed through the room.

"Why, Joy," said Cousin Myrtle, "is it quite right to be playing in that way on Sunday?" for Joy had built herself a queer little hut, the framework of which consisted of the clothes-horse and a couple of high-backed chairs, and had covered it with all the rugs she could find in the library, from the gray badger's skin lined with red flannel that Uncle Ranger had sent home from Wisconsin, to the beautiful Turkish rug that was Uncle Briar's special pride.

Joy popped her curly head from between the curtains of her wigwam. "It's all right, Cousin Myrtle," said she re-assuringly: "it's a holy game. You see our Sunday-school lesson was about the Tabernacle, and I have been building one to see what it looked like. I haven't quite enough curtains. I wish you would let me have your camel's-hair shawl, and — oh! have you got any goat's hair? You know it says that 'all the women whose hearts stirred them up in wisdom spun goat's hair.'"

"The Turkish rug is made of goat's hair," said Uncle Briar, who had followed Myrtle just in time to hear Joy's last request; "and if you will hurry and take that edifice down before aunt returns from church, and come out and swing in the hammock with me, I will tell you a story about it. We will take out the reclining-chair for Cousin Myrtle, and perhaps she will come with us."

So, when they were all fixed out of doors, Uncle Briar went on as follows: —

"Away in Central Asia there lives a wild, nomadic tribe, called the Turcomans. They live just as Jacob and Rachel and Isaac and Rebecca used to. They have camels and horses, and flocks of goats and sheep; and they move about from place to place oftener than fashionable people, who can only stay at Saratoga a few weeks, and must then whisk off to Long Branch for the season there, and then to the White Mountains, changing their location not because they like one place any better than another, but because everybody in their set does so. The Turcomans are very much like our fashionable people: they change their residences in this way, just because their set have always done so. They do not carry great Saratoga trunks around with them; but they carry their houses, and they are nearly as large. Zuleika was a little Turcoman girl, wild and fierce and brave. She had long, straight black hair, and a pretty, oval, olive face. She had no brothers nor sisters, and her only playmate was Mustruf. Mustruf was a silky-haired goat whose milk she drank, and whose hair her mother spun and dyed, and wove in fantastic Oriental patterns, such as her grandmother and great-grandmother and great-great-grandmother had woven. She made mats for their tent and for the top of their cart, to keep the sun from Zuleika's eyes when the cart swayed along over the sand. And Zuleika lay with wide-open, never-winking eyes, staring up at the blending blue, violet, and scarlet, and reading stories of her own from the quaint characters, — spots and bars, and waving lines, that might be the

alphabet of some lost language. Sometimes her mother
wove the golden threads of the silkworm, that looked
like long beams of sunshine streaming through her
fingers; and as she wove she always sang some simple
native melody, with a soul and a meaning in it like that
in Barry Cornwall's 'Weavers' Song,' though the words
were different: —

'Weave, sisters, weave! Swiftly throw
   The shuttle athwart the loom,
And show us how brightly your flowers grow,
   That have beauty, but no perfume.

'Sing, sing, sisters! Weave and sing!
   'Tis good both to sing and to weave;
'Tis better to work than live idle;
   'Tis better to sing than grieve.

'Weave, sisters, weave! Weave and bid
   The colors of sunset glow;
Let grace in each gliding thread be hid;
   Let beauty about ye blow.

Let your skein be long, and your silk be fine,
   And your hands both firm and sure;
And time nor chance shall your work untwine,
   But all — like the truth — endure.'

154

"And then what romps Zuleika had with Mustruf, who was the most intelligent goat in the world! She had all the natural qualities necessary to a trained goat. All she needed was education; for she was far more sagacious than Djali, the performing goat in Victor Hugo's story, 'Notre Dame de Paris,' and could easily have learned the alphabet and to tell the time of day if her mistress had but taught her; but her mistress could not do so, for she had never learned them herself. The goat loved Zuleika, too, with all the affection of which its brute heart was capable, and was often left in charge of her, as a Newfoundland dog might have been.

"There came a time when the great Khan of Khiva and the Emperor of Russia thought that Mustruf and Zuleika had frolicked, and Zuleika's mother woven, long enough; and so, between them, they organized a war involving in suffering and death thousands of other beings as innocent and ignorant as Zuleika and her goat.

"There was a terrible battle in the desert. Zuleika's mother watched it from an oasis, standing in the cart in which Zuleika and Mustruf were curled up together.

She could see nothing but a great swirling cloud of dust, when suddenly from its midst wheeled a band of dusky horsemen: the Turcomans were fleeing. She watched a little longer: swart arms were tossed in the air, and their owners rolled from their horses lifeless to the ground. Suddenly she started, leaped from the cart, and, quite forgetful of Zuleika, ran with bounding leaps straight through the advancing Cossacks toward one of the prostrate men. And Zuleika and Mustruf lay and waited. The battle raged around them, and, with great frightened eyes, they saw it through the rents in the gay, rugs that covered their cart. By and by the tumult ceased, for the battle had swept on. Zuleika called her mother, but she did not come. Women were weeping over their dead in carts near by, but no one came to them. Zuleika was hungry. She took down her little gourd, milked Mustruf, drank, and then, because there was nothing else to do, waited again. The stars came out, and she drew a little rug over herself, and fell asleep. Morning came, and she found herself quite alone; for Mustruf had gone away in search of some one, and the people in the neighboring carts had fled during the night. She climbed down out of the cart, and running a little way stepped upon a sabre that lay half hidden in the sand, and gashed her bare foot badly. Even then the brave little thing did not cry, but limped painfully back to the cart, and sat down again wounded and desolate. But Mustruf had not deserted her mistress, and in her dumb way was working for her better, perhaps, than a human friend could have done.

" The chief of a tribe with whom the Russians were on friendly terms had encamped not far from the field of battle; and one of the officers had been sent by the Russians to make an official call upon him. Now, I should never have known any thing about this story, if this officer, Major Makinoff, had not happened to be an old friend of mine; for he it was who told me all about it when I met him the next summer in Paris. And who was it that told Major Makinoff? Why, Mustruf, to be sure. As the major alighted from his horse, and entered the sheik's *kibitka*, or tent, Mustruf, whose more than instinct had told her where the nearest assemblage of human beings was to be found, trotted into the encampment, and followed him into the presence of the great man. Major Makinoff noticed his companion, but supposed, from her excessive familiarity, that she was a pet of the sheik's. The sheik was somewhat surprised at his visitor, but concluded, as she came with the officer, that she belonged to him, and was perhaps to be offered as a present; and both were too polite to make any remark about the shaggy intruder. But Mustruf, though she was a true scape-goat, had no intention of being used as a peace-offering; and, when she saw that no attention was paid to her, she began to force herself upon their notice. She made a furious charge upon the major just as he rose to make a little speech, running between his legs, and knocking him down. The sheik was too well versed in Oriental etiquette even to smile; and Major Makinoff felt that it would not do to be angry with a favorite of the chief, no matter what liberties she might feel inclined to take: so he picked himself up, with a smile, and remarked that much was to be permitted to the pets of princes; and the sheik, though he did not understand the remark, bowed gravely. The major went on with his oration; and Mustruf, after careering madly three times about the tent, knocked over a tall, gracefully shaped metal pitcher, containing coffee, which stood near the sheik's feet. Fortunately it was not hot, and the sheik was not

scalded; but his yellow satin cushion was stained, and
he scowled visibly.

"Major Makinoff ventured the observation that some
people liked goats. The sheik replied that he did, but
only when they kept their places. 'Then, why don't
you teach yours manners?' asked the major.

"'My goat!' exclaimed the sheik in surprise. 'I never
saw the creature before. I supposed you brought it
here.'

"'And I wondered if you kept the beast on purpose
to insult your visitors; for of course I thought it was
yours,' said Major Makinoff, rising, and assisting the
attendants to drive poor Mustruf off. But, like Mary's
little lamb, Mustruf still lingered near, and waited
patiently about till the major did appear: then it followed
him contentedly as long as his course lay toward Zuleika's cart. But, when he turned aside to ride in another
direction, Mustruf planted herself in his way, and quite
frightened his horse by her ridiculous charges and dancing. Major Makinoff saw that something was really the
matter with the animal; and he reined in his horse, and
waited for an explanation. Then Mustruf would run a
little way toward the oasis, and, returning, repeat her odd

gambols; and the major decided to follow her a little way, and see if he could ascertain what she meant. They had not far to go; and the major, riding to the cart, lifted out the little wounded Zuleika. But even then she took him for an enemy, and resisted all she could, biting and scratching fiercely. He spoke to her very gently and re-assuringly; but she understood Mustruf's actions best, which said as plainly as could be, ' I have brought you a friend.' And she finally allowed herself to be lifted to the saddle, and carried away to the Russian camp.

" Here the surgeon dressed her foot; and the major tended her in his own tent, becoming greatly attached to her, and determining to adopt her as his own daughter, and carry her back to Russia with him. But Mustruf spoiled the plan; for one day, among some haggard women who haunted the camp, demanding that their lost relatives should be restored to them, she recognized Zuleika's mother, and led her by the same dumb pantomime to Major Makinoff's tent. Zuleika and she sprang into each other's arms. It needed no interpreter to explain their relationship; and, without even thanking the major for his care of her child, Zuleika's mother marched her away, Mustruf jogging along in their rear with a perfectly self-satisfied expression of countenance.

"Zuleika's mother *was* grateful, though; and she showed her thanks in deeds instead of words, before the Major left for Russia, bringing him one day a roll of Turkish rugs, each one representing a year's labor. There were five in all,—one for each year of Zuleika's life. Major Makinoff accepted the rugs; but he insisted on paying for them in silver coin, which will probably form a part of Zuleika's marriage-portion some day.

"When he told me this story in Paris, I was so much interested that he gave me one of the rugs: so here you have not only a specimen of Zuleika's mother's skill in weaving, but also a souvenir of Mustruf, composed from many locks of the hair of the faithful goat."

DADDY WORTHLESS

DAR'S bressing in baptizing
      drops,
   Dey dribes de Debble out;
   De rain dat falls upon de
      fields,
      It makes de taters sprout.
   Den sprinkle, sprinkle, sprinkle,
      While de bells go tinkle, tinkle:
   Swing low, old chariot,
      We'll dribe old Satan out."

The long, steep streets of Nashville glowed
   With white dust, parched and dry;
The wind like a sirocco scorched;
   Like copper glared the sky.
A ghastly form strode through the town,
   And at each fireside stood;
It paused at door of rich and poor,
   To trace its sign of blood.

163

Nashville held many heroes brave,
    And ladies fair and gay;
But each man's lip was blanched with fear,
    And mirth all fled away.
Grim Cholera reaped her harvest down,
    And faster toiled each day;
While none could turn her sickle back,
    And none her march could stay.

Young Doctor Starr worked day and night —
    Martyr of science he —
To trace the sources of the blight,
    And what its cause might be.
One night he started from his desk,
    Pushed back his microscope,
And from his laboratory strode,
    All fresh inspired with hope.

" The seeds of death are in the air,
    And we must beat them down:
Oh for refreshing showers of rain!
    E'en now they'd save the town.
I'll lay my plans before the Board
    Of Health at break of day."

The morrow came; and Doctor Starr
   The cholera's victim lay.
Only a negro, gray and old,
   Bent o'er his master's bed,
And listened carefully to all
   He in delirum said.

" Dey calls me Daddy Wufless," thought
   The negro to himself:
" Dey 'll take back dat ar name before
   I'se laid upon de shelf.
I 'd like to spite ole Satan once :
   He thinks to him I'll go ;
But I has got some money saved
   In an ole stockin' toe.
I t'ought dat dat ar money might
   My freedom-papers buy ;
But when a man sees duty clar,
   And sneaking lets it lie,
It had been better for dat man,
   As Judas Scarrot said,
If he 'd been frown into de sea,
   A meal-sack roun' his head.

And so the old man's money bought
    A horse and water-cart;
And every day he drove about
    The city streets and mart,
Till sick men, tossing on their beds
    Of fever and of pain,
Said, as they feebly raised their heads, —
    " I hear the sound of rain,
As when, in nights of childhood past,
    Upon the roof and pane:
The air is fresher than it was,
    And I can breathe again."

The last in every funeral train,
    His water-cart passed by;
And, as he went, he often sang,
    With thin voice cracked and high, —

" Dar 's bressing in baptizing drops,
    Dey dribes de Debble out;
De rain dat falls upon de fields,
    It makes de taters sprout.

Den sprinkle, sprinkle, sprinkle,
While de bells go tinkle, tinkle :
 Swing low, ole chariot,
 We'll dribe ole Satan out."

The scourge is lifted from the town;
 But he who died for it
Lies buried, like a faithful hound,
 Beside his master's feet.
And when I tread that burial-ground
 The tears unbidden start,
To honor " Daddy Wufless" and
 The old man's sprinkling-cart.

PISCES

DICK'S FISH STORY

DICK BRAGG had a wonderful imagination. He did not really mean to tell lies; but every fact that came under his observation was so exaggerated and changed in his report, that it was hardly the same thing. Trifling incidents became terrible calamities, good fortune was magnified in the same ratio, every thing was a great deal worse or a great deal better than it really was. It seemed as if he wore a pair of internal magnifying-glasses that made him see things larger than they actually were; and his whole arithmetic was a table of multiplication. If he found a nest of five or six eggs in the barn, he would say there was about a bushel. He reported that there were millions of potato-bugs on one

of the hills; and when his father made him pick them
off, and count them, he could only find forty. He said
that it was hot enough to melt lead in the hayfield; and
his sister found a little pat of butter in his dinner-pail,
which had returned nearly as solid as it went out. He
was sure there were a thousand peaches on his tree;
and was triumphant when they were gathered to find
that there was a " hundred *anyhow*."

All this might have passed for a very unfortunate
mental disorder, if it had been only a tendency to exag-
geration. It might have been said that he was not
accountable for giving false impressions, if these were
the ones that he received. But Dick sometimes made
stories out of whole cloth, that needed a great deal of
explanation to take the lie out of them. Why these
works of fiction should be called fish-stories, I cannot
say, unless it is that anglers have a temptation to boast
of large catches. But, at all events, no superannuated
whaler sunning himself on the beach was fuller of these
fishy-flavored stories than Dick.

Suddenly there was a great change in him; and no
one was more particular than Dick that the impressions
he gave others should be correct. This was how it

came about. He lived upon the seashore; and there came to board at his father's house, one summer, a very peculiar gentleman. He had been a sea-captain, but had left the sea after having gained a large fortune. He was not a happy man, in spite of his wealth; for, while away on his last voyage, he had met with a loss that took away all the enjoyment from life. His wife had died. His only child, a little girl, had been taken away by an aunt, of whom, strange to say, he could find no trace, though he had spared no pains or expense in the search. He had given it up now, and would sit for hours in a reclining-chair on the piazza, looking off at the sea with an expression of despondency that it was pitiful to see on the face of a strong man in the prime of life. Sometimes he would rouse from his melancholy, and talk with Dick, whose bright replies interested him; and Dick, emboldened by the gentleman's attention, would relate the most impossible adventures, of the truth of which his hearer never expressed the slightest doubt, listening quietly, with an amused smile now and then creeping across his face.

"You will be telling me some yarn about Capt. Kidd next," he said one day.

"Who was he?" asked Dick.

"A pirate who sailed and sailed, and who is said to have left untold treasures buried at various points along our coast. There are few seaports that haven't their legends of sacks of gold hidden somewhere by him; but no one has been fortunate enough to find them yet."

Dick was quiet for some time, for his busy brain was at work. "Capt. Starboard," said he after a pause, "I should not wonder if that old pirate you mentioned just now *did* have a cave or something near here; for I know a little girl whose mother found lots and lots of guineas somewhere along the coast."

"Dick, Dick!" said Capt. Starboard reprovingly.

"Yes, she did, though," persisted the boy. "And they weren't tied up in bags nor nothing neither; and she lives on 'em now, honest Injun."

"Honest Injun" was Dick's most solemn affirmation. When he said that, and looked you straight in the face with his one gray and one blue eye, you might be sure that it was equivalent to an oath at court, and that what he said was the unvarnished truth or — that it was a great deal bigger lie than usual. Capt. Starboard looked at Dick thoughtfully. "I must inquire into this," he said

to himself, "and, if the boy has no grounds for his assertion, see if something cannot be done to correct this bad
habit."

As far as words went, Dick had been speaking the
truth; but Capt. Starboard had not understood him
correctly, as Dick had intended he should not; and,
as sin consists in an intention to do wrong, Dick had
told a downright lie. The truth was this: At a lonely
house down on Sandy Cove, lived a poor old woman,
who had come to the place some three years before,
and who earned a scanty living by doing washing.
She had a little girl strangely delicate and beautiful,
quite unlike the rough mother, though each seemed
exceedingly fond of the other. Dick had seen her when
he had been sent to the house with clothes, and had
struck up quite an intimacy with the lonely little thing.
Once when he came he did not find her. "Where is
Floy?" he asked of the woman.

"Oh, I found a flock of guineas," she replied; "and
Floy is up on the hill taking care of them. I expect
they strayed from some farm near here. If you hear of
any one having lost them, let me know."

Dick climbed the sandy bank, and found Floy in the

meadow watching the guinea-fowls that were stepping stiffly about in the grass. They were quite shy of him; but they allowed Floy to come near to them, and a few were even bold enough to eat from her hand.

" They are so pretty," said she, "and I think they look real stylish. Mamma used to have a dress like that with white polka spots in it, only the ground was black instead of gray: it was trimmed with black lace, I remember. My papa brought it to her from some foreign country. It was some sort of gauzy stuff, and she wore it over a long black silk skirt; and you don't know how beautiful she looked with the starry chrysanthemums in her black hair."

" But your mamma has red hair," said Dick.

" I know this mamma has, but my other one didn't use to," persisted the child.

Not long afterward it was ascertained that the guinea-fowls belonged to a kind-hearted farmer for whom the old woman did washing. But they had become so much attached to their new home that they would not return; and the farmer seeing that Floy would be nearly heart-broken if they were taken away, and feeling just then remarkably good-natured from having sold his hay-

crop to good advantage, made her a present of them.
After this Floy was not quite so lonely; for her guineas,
as she called them, were companions as well as a source
of income for her.

This was what Dick had in mind when he told Capt.
Starboard his remarkable fish-story about the guineas;
and the captain had replied, " I wish you would tell me
where this old woman lives who found the gold. I
should like to see if any traces can be found of Capt.
Kidd in this region."

Dick started. He had not expected that his story
would be put to the test; but his love of fun triumphed
over the dislike of being detected in deception. It
would be such a good joke to set the captain on a wild-
goose chase after relics of Capt. Kidd! With a little
enlargement it would make the grandest kind of a story
to tell at school that winter; and so he directed him
carefully to the house of the washerwoman at Sandy
Cove, and with the greatest inward glee watched the
apparently unsuspecting gentleman set out upon his
expedition.

Capt. Starboard little thought, as he knocked at the
door, that he was on the verge of discovering a treasure

more precious to him than a hundred chests of golden guineas.

"Rachel!" he exclaimed in astonishment, as the hard-visaged, red-haired woman met him. "How did you come here?" For this strange creature was the ignorant but faithful nurse that he had left with his wife and baby daughter when he set out on his last voyage. And Rachel between her sobs told the whole sad story of how Mrs. Starboard had died, and her sister who had come to nurse her had taken them away, intending to share her own home with them until Capt. Starboard returned, but was stricken down by the same disease on the way, and died in a strange city. Then Rachel had tried to return to the town they had left, but in her ignorance had bought a ticket to the wrong place, and found herself penniless here. She could not write, and could think of no friends to whom to apply; and so in her uncomplaining fortitude and stout-heartedness she had determined to stay here until she could earn enough to take her home, hoping that by that time she would find out somehow where home was.

This was the explanation, but it did not all come at once; for, in the first part of it, Capt. Starboard had

caught sight of flaxen-haired little Floy peering wonder-
ingly at him from behind the wash-tubs. She had outgrown any likeness to the baby that he had left; but she
had acquired instead a remarkable resemblance to her
mother. And the captain caught her in his arms with a
great cry of joy. He could not speak for a while, but
held her upon his knee, stroking her silky hair, while
great tears rolled down his face. When he found his
voice at last, it was in prayer, the first that he had
uttered since his loss. And then he sobbed aloud again,
called her his own, own little girl, and declared that she
should not stay another hour at Sandy Cove.

"Come, Rachel," he said. "It will not take you long
to pack, and we shall be in time for the afternoon train.
I am impatient to show Floy to her old friends."

"But, papa," said Floy, "what shall we do with the
guineas?"

"Then you really did find some guineas on the beach?
Dick Bragg told me so; but I thought it was all a fish-
story, and that the young scamp was fooling me. How
many are there left?"

"Twenty, papa."

"Well, pet, I should like to make Dick a very handsome present; for he has brought us together again. What do you say to letting nurse carry up the guineas to him, since I have money enough for us both? She can tell his father at the same time to send my trunk to the depot.

"I like Dick very much. He is a bright boy, and, I am told, one of the best scholars at the district school. He confided to me that it was the ambition of his life to go to college; but he did not think his father could ever afford it. He said that he was saving up all his spending-money toward that end. I think his hoard amounts now to one dollar and sixty-five cents; and the guineas will be an important addition."

A half-hour later, Dick was astonished at receiving the following note: —

MASTER DICK BRAGG, — I am glad to find that you have told me the truth, and you will not be sorry to learn that little Floy is my lost lassie. I send you by the bearer of this note one hundred and twenty dollars, *English money*, which I am sure will be rightly expended.

With sincere regard, yours,

N. E. STARBOARD.

One hundred and twenty dollars! He turned faint, and every thing whirled about him. He could go to college next year! He could scarcely see Rachel through the blur that gathered over his eyes. She recalled him to himself with the remark, " The guineas are in the garden." That was a strange place to leave money! And, hatless and breathless, he rushed out only to see the detestable fowls destroying his mother's flower-bed.

It was his last fish-story.

PEEP THE LAST.

THE TAIL OF A COMET.

MONG the wonderful Bayeux tapestries which have been handed down through the centuries, to tell of the exploits of William the Conqueror, and of the patience and skill of the ladies of his court who thus recorded them, there is one that represents the army marching to victory, led by a brilliant comet.

"The comet had more to do with the expulsion of the Danes, the end of the Saxon rule in England, and the establishment of Norman rule there, than history gives it credit for, or than usually falls to the lot of these flame-birds from the Sky-Garden.

"Hundreds of years ago, during the reign of Edward the Confessor in England, there lived across the Channel, in the Province of Normandy, a great duke named William. His wife Matilda was a very remarkable woman; and their children, of whom five were girls and three boys, were accomplished in all the arts of the age. Cicily, the eldest daughter, was pure and stately as a lily. She had been consecrated from her birth to the church, and afterward became abbess of the Convent of the Holy Trinity at Caen. She was still at home; but the shadow of her approaching separation from her family rested upon her, and kept her more constantly than her other sisters at her mother's knee, while looks of tenderness and frequent caresses passed between them. Constantia, the beauty of the family, had just been married to Alan Fergaut, the great Earl of Brittany, and had gone away, a happy bride, to her husband's castle. She was sadly missed at home, for she was as lovely in disposition as in feature; while her witty and brilliant conversation led her father to call her the central rose-diamond in his coronet of girls. Alice, the third daughter, did not by any means take her place, for she was shy as well as wilful, and plain of feature, com-

pared with her handsome sisters. Adela, her younger
sister, a rosebud girl hardly more than a child, was
already betrothed to Stephen, Earl of Blois, — and Blois
was one of the most beautiful cities and richest earldoms
in the South of France. But Alice had never had a
suitor; and she combed her straight black hair smoothly
back under her little Norman cap, with the bitter feeling
at heart, that no one, even here in her father's house,
cared very much for her, and that tiny Agatha had
already, in her short life, found more of love than she.

Into this family, at the time that our story begins,
there came a visitor, young Harold the Saxon, brother-
in-law of the King of England. Duke William informed
him of his design of claiming the English crown, on the
death of the king; and Harold took the most solemn
oaths to support his claims. The blue eyes and yellow
hair of the stalwart Saxon formed a striking contrast to
the appearance of the more polished but less manly
Norman knights with whom Alice was familiar. Their
guest seemed more heroic than any one she had yet
seen; while, to Harold, shy Alice was more pleasing
than any of the Duke's handsome daughters. He loved
to sit in the oriel window, and hold the skeins of violet

silk that she wound; or watch the slender form droop over the tapestry-frame, on which the deft white fingers moved swiftly backward and forward. Sometimes, when he talked of England, there was a swift lifting of the long, fringy lashes, and an interested look in the dark eyes; and both Harold and Alice bent readily to the will of the Duke, which betrothed them to each other. As they stood together one evening, in the window, under the sparkling starlight of a Norman night, looking away toward the stormy sea that Harold was soon to recross, Alice looked at him so fixedly that he became uneasy, and asked her what she meant by so earnest a gaze.

"'The starlight lets me look down through your eyes to your soul,' she replied; 'and it is not all open and clear there. You do not love me, Harold, with an undivided heart; and something tells me that you will forget the promises you have made on French soil.'

"But Harold took the cold white hand in his, and, pointing to the sky, said, 'I will be as true as the stars, Alice. When you see one of them wandering about among the fixed constellations, then Harold will wander from his love. When one of heaven's steadfast lights flies away from its place, nevermore to return to its shining companions, then you may doubt that Harold will return. Dry your tears; for I will be true, my Alice,—as true as the stars.'

"Then Harold went away, and the days that followed were long and lonely. Alice's brothers had been her comfort before; but, since her betrothal to the Saxon nobleman, they regarded her as an alien and a stranger; and Short-stockinged Robert and William the Red-head (nicknames which clung to them even after one was a distinguished knight fighting under Godfrey in the Holy Land, and the other had become King of England) suddenly lost all their old sympathy, and became as rude and rough with her as with any one else. Then Edward the Confessor died; and Harold, forgetting his promises to William of Normandy, caused himself to be proclaimed King of England. News came, too, that he had been as false to Alice as to her father, and that he had married a Saxon princess far away in Northumberland.

"'He has broken no promise to me,' said Alice proudly; and she pointed to the skies, where, away in the north, a star was moving among the fixed constellations: and, willing even then to justify and forgive the man who had wronged her so cruelly, she repeated her last conversation with Harold.

"'Wandering stars,' quoted her Uncle Odo, the Archbishop of Bayeux, from his Latin Bible, — 'wandering stars, for whom is reserved the blackness of darkness forever.' But Duke William saw in the comet an augury of success for his cause. He could not forgive Harold as his daughter had done, but adopted the comet as his ensign, and caused to be inscribed upon his banners the motto, '*Nova Stella, Novus Rex,*' — a new star, a new king. Many powerful nobles and celebrated knights came and asked to be allowed to fight under him; and a large and formidable army set out for the conquest of England. While the bold warrior believed that he was following the guidance of the comet in this incursion, his wife Matilda gathered her maids of honor about her in her old château in Normandy, where they beguiled the absence of their fathers, brothers, and lovers by embroidering the wonderful Bayeux tapestries, working the comet in, and representing it as leading the army to victory. We can imagine how these mediæval ladies chatted as they drew the richly tinted silks through the cloth of gold, alternately discussing the new sign in

the heavens, and vaunting the merits of their favorite
knights ; and while one boasted that Eustace Count of
Boulogne was most noble, another replied that Aimeri de
Thonars was bravest, a third declared Roger de Beau-
mont most accomplished and elegant in manners, and
others boasted Hugh de Grantmesriel as wealthiest,
Charles Martel as the perfection of manly beauty, and
William de Warenne as purest and best.

"Alice alone was silent; but we can believe that no
other fingers than hers embroidered the comet, in its
glowing flame-color and gold. Before the tapestry was
completed, news was brought to the castle of the battle
of Hastings, of the defeat of the English, and the death
of Harold. William of Normandy was William the
Conqueror and King of England now. The comet and
Harold had alike vanished, and were forgotten. But we
can guess through whose influence a monastery, called
Battle Abbey, was erected on the field of the bloody
conflict, where prayers were to be offered for Harold's
soul throughout all future time; for the Normans showed
themselves as magnanimous to their conquered enemies
as they were cruel on the field. And the abbey and the
tapestries passed down through the ages, —

'Thanking God, whose boundless wisdom makes the flowers of pardon
    bloom
In the battle's blood and horror, in the tissues of the loom.
Vanished are the story's actors ; but, before my dreamy eye,
Wave these mingling shapes and figures, like a faded tapestry.'"

"And is that all the story?" asked Joy.

"No," replied Uncle Briar; "for this was not the first
or the last time that this comet visited our earth.
Indeed, it has been proved to be an old acquaintance of
ours, who drops in to see us once every seventy-five
years ; and we may consider these calls quite frequent if
we compare them with those of almost any other comet
of our acquaintance. The Chinese have kept an account
of its first visits for us. It was not noticed by the
European nations until the year 837, during the reign of
Louis the Gay, son of the great Emperor Charlemagne.
He was so frightened by its appearance, that he knelt
and prayed to it, and spent the remainder of his life in
building abbeys and cathedrals. In 1456, during the
war with the Mussulmans, it appeared like a flaming
Turkish cimeter in the sky, and was taken as a favorable omen for the Mahometans, who were really successful for some time ; and Pope Calixtus III., to encourage

the Crusaders, excommunicated the comet publicly. One would have thought that it would have been so offended as not to come again; but punctually in 1531 the comet re-appeared; and Louise of Savois, the mother of Francis I., who was lying upon her death-bed, saw it flash through her palace window, and accepted it as the sign of her death. Kepler studied it upon its next visit; and in 1682 Edmund Halley, who was on his way to Paris, observed it again. All the scientific world was interested in the comet now, and set to work on the problem of its period of revolution, or in trying to predict when it would again be seen. Halley was the first who identified it with the one whose appearances I have already mentioned, and foretold its coming correctly. He showed that the comet would not be promptly on time at its next visit, for its track lay near Jupiter and Saturn. And, by a comparison of the masses of these planets with that of the comet, he was enabled to tell that Jupiter would retard it five hundred and eight days, and Saturn one hundred; and so fixed its return on the 13th of April, 1759. Reviewing his work, he admitted that there might be an error in it of a month, and so left it for the future to verify or disprove. How much he must have longed to live until this time, to know the result! But he died an old man, in his chair, without a groan, in 1741. The comet had been prayed to and excommunicated, followed as a symbol of victory, and feared as a foreteller of disaster; but it was not christened until 1759. Then, when on the 12th of March, within the limits which Halley assigned it, the comet really appeared, it was named by unanimous consent, Halley's Comet, — a just tribute to the immense painstaking and accuracy of the astronomer's calculations.

"I owe much that I have told you to Camille Flammarion's 'Stories of Infinity.' But he will lead you farther into the fairy-land of astronomy, telling you what the comet thought of the earth at each visit, and not, as I have done, what the earth thought of the comet.

"You may see the comet for yourself, little Joy; for it will call again in 1911. Look for it, and remember Alice, the daughter of William, who deserved the title of conqueror less than his daughter, for she conquered all revengeful feeling. And, if any one has wronged you, try to forgive them for His sake whose birth was ushered in by the beautiful star in the east."

JOY LOOKING AT ROCKET-STAR

S Joy stood at her window, and once more looked up at the star-bright sky, she was filled with sadness: she was to hear no more stories; for she had just met with a great loss,—Cousin Myrtle and Uncle Briar both taken away from her at one blow. She had known for a long time that it would come to this. There did not seem to be any thing very dreadful then in the mere fact that Uncle Briar loved Cousin Myrtle; and she had never thought of its leading to any thing like this,—of his taking her away from them, and going away himself, "for always." But Uncle Briar had obtained a position in a party of scientific men who were going away to a foreign land to observe the transit of Venus; and he had thought it a favorable opportunity to be married, and take Cousin Myrtle with him. The wedding had been a very grand affair; and as Joy and Bobby Copernicus had been first bridesmaid and first groomsman, and had preceded the bridal party up the broad aisle of the church, standing beside the altar-rail while the mystical words were spoken, and sharing in all the festivities of the evening, being dressed, too, almost as handsomely as Cousin Myrtle, Joy could not divest herself of the idea that *she* had been married to Cousin Myrtle, and constantly spoke of it in this way, to the great amusement of the company, and especially of Uncle Briar, who was quite left out in the cold by this arrangement. All this was only yesterday evening; but now the Chinese lanterns in the garden were all extinguished. Cousin Myrtle's presents, which had loaded the library-table, had been packed away ready to be sent to her new home when she should return from her wedding tour; and Cousin Myrtle and Uncle Briar themselves were far away, enjoying their honeymoon at that commonest and loveliest haunt of newly married couples, Niagara Falls, while they waited for the assembling of the party with which they were to start upon their astronomical mission. Joy could not understand it very clearly. They were going to see the transit of Venus; and yet Uncle Briar had said that Venus had already crossed his pathway, or he should not have been married. But then, Uncle Briar was such a funny man, one could never tell when he was in jest, and when in earnest. Joy had been so lonely all day that in the evening her father, pitying his forlorn little girl, had taken her upon his knee, and read her the ballad of the "Culprit Fay." The last part reminded her very much of the Sky-Garden and of her playfellow Puck; and she thought that if he had loved her as the Fay did the earth-maiden, he would have known that she had lost Cousin Myrtle, and would have come to comfort her ere this.

As the thought passed through her mind, she felt a fairy kiss upon her cheek, — the merest touch, as from rosebud baby lips, and looking up saw Puck at a little distance, bestriding a very strange steed. It had a head like an old man, and at the same time like a star. A white, gauzy veil was thrown over its face, and streamed far back, mingling with its white hair, and quite concealing whatever of body this strange being possessed.

195

Joy's thought flew back to her last star talk with Uncle Briar; and she was not much surprised when Puck introduced his companion as Halley's Comet.

"Come, Joy," said Puck: "this is a beautiful night for a ride. You have only seen a very few of the beauties and marvels of the Sky-Garden. We should never be able to see them all if we walked slowly through it as we did on your last visit; but we can accomplish a great deal on such a swift courser as this. If you had rather ride in a carriage, as you generally do here in this slow world, I will fly up to the sky, and bring down Charles's Chariot, or Charles's Wain, which is the old-fashioned name your father calls it by. But we shouldn't move nearly so fast; and I doubt if you would be any more comfortable."

"Indeed, indeed," protested Joy, "I would much rather go on horseback." And then, seeing by the smile on the comet's face that she had used the wrong term, she added, "Excuse me, sir. I know that you are not a horse; but I didn't know what to call you."

"Never mind," said Puck, holding out his hand to assist her: —

196

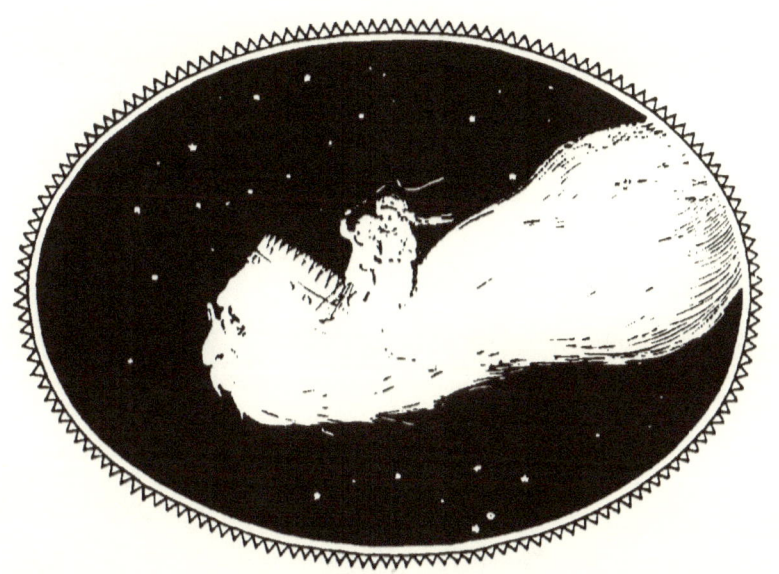

A RIDE ON THE ROCKET-STAR

" ' Mount thy steed, and spur him high
To the heaven's blue canopy ;
And, when thou seest a shooting star,
Follow it fast, and follow it far.' "

Joy seated herself behind Puck, twining her arms
about him, while the phosphorescent trail of the comet
formed a soft but firm pillion beneath her. It was something like Diamond in North Wind's hair, she thought.
And now they darted straight up, up, till they entered
the clouds. They seemed in a region bewitched. Sometimes the shifting cloud-forms parted, and gave her a
glimpse of the earth, falling, falling, away beneath: sometimes they closed about her, rising in gigantic shapes,
but always dim and spectral, though they threw dashes
of real spray in her face, as Kuhlborn the water-sprite
did to Undine when he followed her through the forest.
The light was that noticed by Herschel in his description of Halley's comet,—"a light that never shone on
sea or land." Sky there was none. There seemed to
be nothing beyond but solid banks of rainbow-streaked
mother-of-pearl. And yet these shimmering phantoms
of the upper air did not in the least depress Joy: they
seemed to be spirits of the grotesque,—fun etherealized ;

and she told herself how exactly like the "Culprit Fay"
it all was. And, while she rested her chin on Puck's
warm shoulder, she repeated to him as much as she
could remember of the poem, telling how —

> " Up to the vaulted firmament,
>   His path the fire-fly courser bent.
>   He flies like a feather in the blast
>   Till the first light cloud in heaven is past ;
>   But the shapes of air have begun their work,
>   And a drizzly mist is round him cast ;
>   He cannot see through the mantle murk :
>   He shivers with cold, but he urges fast ;
>   Through storm and darkness, sleet and shade,
>   He lashes his steed, and spurs amain,
>   For shadowy hands have twitched the rein,
>   And flame-shot tongues around him played.
>   His eyes are blurred with the lightning's glare,
>   And his ears are stunned with the thunder's blare."

Till —

> " Howling the misty spectres flew :
>   They rend the air with frightful cries,
>   For he has gained the welkin blue,
>   And the land of clouds beneath him lies."

As Joy repeated the last line, the cloudy gates of pearl

flew open. (They were the same as the ivory gate that old Virgil told about when he said, —

    " Sleep gives its name to portals twain ;

    And one that bright with ivory gleams
    Whence Pluto sends delusive dreams."

But Joy did not know this, for she had not begun to study Virgil yet; and she would have felt badly enough if she had known that her ride on the rocket star was all a delusive dream.) With the opening of the gates, Joy found herself once more in the enchanted Sky-Garden.

"Are we going through the Zodiac?" she asked; for she recognized the constellation Taurus, just where she was when Bobby Copernicus waked her from her last delightful ramble with Puck.

"No," replied the elfin jockey: "the comet will pursue the same course that it did when last observed from the earth. Even comets do not wander about by chance as some people think. They have their route marked out for them, and always obey orders: if they did not, Halley would not have been able to tell when this very one would arrive."

199

" It must be stupid enough," said Joy musingly.

" What must be stupid?" asked Puck.

" To always have to be on time, just like a railroad engineer or a schoolgirl. And it seems to me that Mr. Comet was tardy the time that Halley told about, and played truant with Jupiter and Saturn for ever so long."

" No: because things do not always happen in just the same way, is no reason that they are not ordered and arranged beforehand just the same. Saturn is a comet ruler, and the comet was told to do his errands for a time. It was late at school; but it did not receive a tardy-mark, for its excuse was all written out, and Halley knew it. Do you happen to know where you are now, little Miss Joy?"

" Yes," replied Joy; " that is, I think we are among the Pleiades. Uncle Briar said I could see them upon the meridian ten minutes before nine any New Year's night. And that V-shaped cluster in the bull's face is the Hyades, is it not?"

" Yes. But do you know the names of the Pleiades, and who they were?" asked Puck.

" No," replied Joy. " Were they not always stars?"

" They were all girls once, the Greek mythology tells

us; and their names were Alcyone, Merope, Maia, Electra, Tayeta, Sterope, and Celeno. But they were all so lovely and good that they were allowed to come up into the Sky-Garden, not just for a little ride such as you are taking, but to live here always; and, if you are very good indeed, you can too: though I suppose you don't believe a word I am saying, just because you never heard it at your Sunday school."

"But I have heard it there," said Joy. "The minister said so last Sunday."

"He did, eh?" exclaimed Puck in surprise. "Then he must be a much more sensible man than most ministers: that's all."

"And they that be wise," repeated Joy "shall shine as the brightness of the firmament; and they that turn many to righteousness, as the stars for ever and ever." And, as they swept away from the Pleiad sisters, Joy sang to them, as she had done at sabbath school a few days before, —

"O ye stars! shine on
Far up in heaven's own blue:
Some time, some time, I too shall shine,
I shall shine as brightly as you."

"You are a queer little girl," said Puck.

Onward and still onward sped the comet between the constellation of the Twins and that of Auriga the charioteer, who Puck said was no other than Phaeton, thrown here when attempting, like some inexperienced young London blood, to drive the Sun's great twenty-four-in-hand. The thought of the accident made Joy shudder, and cling closer to Puck, though Auriga looked contented enough where he sat with the Kids in his lap. They had passed into the kingdom of the Lynx now; and Joy looked the savage animal bravely in the eye, — that strange eye formed of a gold and purple double star. She was near enough to his mouth to see the triple star in his lower jaw, shining orange, blue, and garnet.

"We are just behind Charles's Wain now." said Puck ; "and it started long before we did. You can see what a slow coach it is compared to our lightning express."

Joy shaded her eyes with her hand, and peered forward. "Why, it is only the Dipper!" said she.

"Call it by what name you like," replied Puck. "The ancients called it the Plough, and some call it the Great Bear ; it can be any and all of these, and my favorite plat of star-flowers at the same time. I don't know that it makes any difference what you mortals call the stars.

"The man that I knew best in your world, and the one whose opinion I have the greatest respect for, — gentle Will Shakspeare, — loved them right loyally, but did not care for their names. He used to say of astronomers, —

> 'Those earthly godfathers of heaven's lights,
> That give a name to every fixèd star,
> Have no more profit of their shining nights
> Than those that walk, and know not what they are.'"

"I think that Mr. Shakspeare was wrong," said Joy modestly. "I am sure, the more we know about any thing, the more we enjoy it. But see, we are following right on in the track of Charles's Chariot, as you call it. This is just the way that the Culprit Fay went. There is one verse which just describes us now : - -

> 'Borne afar on the wings of the blast,
> Northward away they speed them fast :
> And their courser follows Charles's Wain
> Till their hoof-strokes fall like pattering rain,
> While swiftly follows in their flight
> The streaming of the rocket-light.'"

But the comet was swifter than the great wagon, and they soon passed it, nodding kindly, as they went by, to Boötes the bear-driver, and taking a look next at the resplendent northern crown; but, before they turned their faces southward, Puck stopped to see that the Pole-star was securely fastened to its slender staff.

"You shall come with me on some great *fête* night, and see the wonderful dance," said Puck. "This is the best place from which to watch it;" and he led her into the Pole-star pavilion, whose

> "Spiral columns gleaming bright
> Were streamers of the northern light."

How beautiful the stately lily-star looked as seen through the rose-colored arches that surrounded it! Joy had seen it often from the earth, between the fluttering pink silk curtains that fell from the spiral columns; but it had only seemed a star to her then, with streaks of pale light wavering about it. Now it was all so much plainer, so much more beautiful! "What dance do you mean?" she asked, turning to Puck with wistful eyes.

"The dance of the angels," replied Puck quite seriously.

"But it is wicked to dance," said Joy; "and I am sure the angels never do so."

"But Milton, who knew more, or at least wrote more, about the angels than any one else, says they do," persisted Puck. "He tells of one day which, —

> 'As other solemn days they spent
> In song and dance about the sacred hill ;
> Mystical dance, which yonder starry sphere
> Of planets and of stars in all her wheels
> Resembles nearest.'"

Their comet ride was almost ended. They darted on between Hercules and Serpentarius down into Ophiuchus, the symbol of the healing art, telling its starry allegory of how those who spend their lives in alleviating human suffering, in lifting away the serpents of sin and pain and poverty and ignorance that coil about their helpless brothers, shall finally have their place in the heavens; and the comet had finished the visible path which it had traversed on its last earthly appearance.

"I want to take you now," said Puck, "to a part of the star-garden so distant that if we should go and return on the comet it would be years before we should reach the earth again; and your father and mother would be anxious and sad enough if they found you had vanished away like Kilmeny. We must travel in some faster way. There is the lightning now: how would you like to take a ride on that?"

"Not a bit," said Joy with a shudder. "It must be very dreadful indeed, especially if the thunder goes along too."

"I did not think you would like it," said Puck; "and then, after all, it isn't fast enough either."

"Why, what can go faster than lightning?"

"A thought-beam; and we will travel on one of them. You can pass over millions of miles in a second on a thought."

As he spoke, Joy caught a last glimpse of the rocket-star vanishing in the distance; but she never forgot her wonderful ride, and could point out for you now, if you asked her, either in the heavens or on a celestial globe, the track of Halley's Comet.

"What are you thinking about?" asked Puck suddenly.

"I was only saying a foolish little rhyme to myself," said Joy blushing; and she repeated, —

"Star bright, star light, the first star I've seen to-night,
I wish I may, I wish I might, have the wish I wish to-night."

"Well, that is foolish in good earnest," said Puck, laughing. "The first star, indeed! when you've seen thousands of them. Well, what did you wish?"

"I wished that I could see something that was passing on our earth," said Joy.

"That is just like you mortals," replied Puck, "always wishing for something you haven't got. When you were on the earth, you wanted a nearer view of the Sky-Garden; and, now that you are here, you want to look at the earth. Though, come to think of it, your request is not so nonsensical, after all; for some things do look better from a distance: and so, if you like, I will show you a set of heliotypes."

"What! do they have them up here?" asked Joy in surprise.

"What *are* heliotypes?" retorted Puck.

"Why, a sort of photograph. Father has lots of them at home in a portfolio."

"Nonsense! Heliotypes are sun-pictures, that's all; and the light is a sort of postman that carries and delivers them wherever it goes. Now, if you look just in the direction that I point, you will see a heliotype of the earth."

" It is so very small," said she, quite disappointed.

"One should never look at heliotypes without a magnifying-glass," replied Puck, offering her his own.

Joy uttered a little scream of delight. "I can see our very own house," said she, "with the observatory on the roof, and father at the transit, and — why, if there isn't Uncle Briar and Cousin Myrtle, as large as life ! Have they really come back so soon ? "

" If you had read Camille Flammarion's stories, you would not make that mistake," replied her companion. "What you see is not what is happening on the earth now, but what happened a week ago."

"How can that be ? " asked Joy.

" An astronomer's daughter ought to know that light does not pass from place to place instantaneously, any more than sound or your earthly postman. It takes nearly nine minutes to reach your earth from the sun. Now, we are many thousand times farther off from the earth than the sun is, and consequently it takes the light a much longer time to reach us ; and the pictures which he brings are of things that happened some time

LIGHT CARRYING HELIOTYPES·

since. It is not quite so bad here, however, as it was with the man who lived in Southern Africa, where it took sailing-vessels six months to come to him from his home, so that all of his newspapers and letters were six months old; though Light has some places that take him quite as long to reach, for his postman's round is a long one."

Joy had not been listening to the last part of what Puck had been saying. She seemed very much interested in what she saw; and she now exclaimed, " Why, I can see *me*, my ownty-donty self, walking around! How very funny!" Suddenly her face displayed an expression of extreme vexation.

" That was the day I told the lie," she said; "such a mean lie too. I wish Light would not go on making me say it over again. I am sure I am sorry enough for it; and I didn't want you, Puck, to know I had ever done any thing so wicked."

" Being sorry is good," said Puck, " but it does not make the matter all right again. . Light tells every thing. He is worse than the daily newspaper, because every one knows that he never slanders or exaggerates, but that every thing he tells is strictly true; and the trouble of it is, that he tells every thing, and tells it everywhere, so that, no matter what naughty thing we do, Light carries heliotypes of it from star to star, from world to world, and keeps on carrying them for ever and ever."

"And can any one who comes to the Sky-Garden see them? When Uncle Briar and Cousin Myrtle come, will they know?"

Puck nodded sadly. "There will not be a spot in the Sky-Garden where Light will not have left this helio-type. Your friends will probably be as interested as you are in seeing what is passing on the earth; and, if they love you, they will take pleasure in going just to that spot where Light will spread your whole life before them."

"Oh! I never can look them in the face again, never!" said Joy, covering her crimson cheeks with her hands. "To think that they will sit and see me do that mean thing over again, and maybe I be with them too, and be obliged to see myself disgrace myself before the people I love best! Oh! it is too much."

"Do not cry so," said Puck soothingly, "but try to be more careful in future what heliotypes you let Light carry away to the Sky-Garden. Let there be so many of real repentance for this wrong act, and so many of beautiful deeds done secretly, that your friends in looking them over, and remembering the sin and weakness of their own lives, will be able to forgive this black one, and to love you as much, when they know all, as they do now. It will take a great deal of resolution to remember this always. But there is one star that is a symbol of will; and you can let it be a reminder to you, as well as a comfort, whenever you see it."

"What star is it?" asked Joy.

"It is the planet Mars," replied Puck. "Did you never read Longfellow's poem about it? You see, I know all the poets, for they all know me. I want you to learn the whole poem as soon as you reach home. But I will repeat a few verses from it now, that you may be sure you have found the one I mean: —

> 'There is no light in earth or heaven,
>   But the cold light of stars ;
> And the first watch of night is given
>   To the red planet Mars.

'The star of the unconquered will,
   He rises in my breast
Serene and resolute and still,
   And calm and self-possessed.

'And thou too, whosoe'er thou art,
   That readest this brief psalm,
As one by one thy hopes depart,
   Be resolute and calm.

'Oh, fear not in a world like this,
   And thou shalt know ere long, —
Know how sublime a thing it is
   To suffer and be strong.' "

"I will try to remember," said Joy, wiping her eyes. "But, oh! I would so like to see Uncle Briar and Cousin Myrtle just for two minutes!"

"Then you need not look toward the earth any longer; for they are not there," replied Puck.

"Why! where can they be, then?"

"In the moon, to be sure."

"In the moon!"

"Yes, in the honey-moon. When people get married, they are usually carried to the moon to live, for a while at least; some people never get there at all, and some

IN THE HONEY-MOON

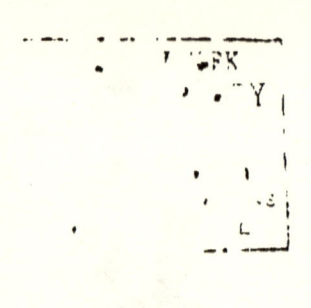

never get back. There are your father and mother; they have gone on living in the moon ever since they were married, and there is not the slightest doubt that they will remain there permanently."

" I know Cousin Myrtle used to be very fond of the moon," said Joy thoughtfully. " She modelled the principal craters in wax for Uncle Briar; and she used to quote all sorts of sentimental poetry about it; and, my! didn't she use to like to take moonlight walks, though ! "

" Take my magnifying-glass, and look at the moon now," said Puck, "and you will see them. Do you remember the names of any of the localities in the moon ? Though perhaps your cousin did not see fit to explain them to you as she modelled them."

" Oh ! yes, she did," exclaimed Joy. " I remember the Lake of Dreams, especially, and the Sea of Serenity too."

" The Lake of Dreams, — hum ! that's where they are now. All young married people go there first; but they never stay long. They either drop right out of the moon as soon as it changes from full to crescent, or else pass on to the shores of the Sea of Serenity, as your parents did. The moon is a royal queen-mother to all children, and to all people with childlike hearts. You know how full Mother Goose is of moon-stories. The sweetest lullaby that was ever written says, —

> ' Sleep, baby, sleep :
> The great stars are the sheep ;
> The little stars are the lambs, I guess ;
> And the white moon is the shepherdess.'

Among grown-up people, only poets and lovers, astronomers and lunatics, care for the moon ; only very happy or very sad, very wise or very silly people. You never hear commonplace folks talking about it ; they seem to think that it is a sign of weakness to care for her : but the great and powerful ocean, that no human might can control, that kills strong men who dare to come near it in its fits of fury, follows the moon like a little child, and obeys her rule as though it were an abject slave. That is what it is to exert an influence, little Joy. One may not be very powerful of one's self, and yet may influence some giant nature in some way that we never thought of. It is not the great world alone that has an atmosphere : every heavy-headed poppy and every sweet rose has one."

Suddenly Puck started. " Day glimmers in the east," he said: "if you do not return to your earthly home soon, you cannot go at all. But oh, Joy, why do you go? You have not seen half the wonders of the Sky-Garden.

'Return no more to your woodland height,
   But ever here with me abide
In the land of everlasting light:
   Within the fleecy drift we'll lie ;
We'll hang upon the rainbow's rim ;
   And all the jewels of the sky
Around thy brow shall brightly beam';
And thou shalt bathe thee in the stream
   That rolls its whitening foam aboon,
And ride upon the lightning's gleam,
   And dance upon the orbèd moon ;
We'll sit within the Pleiad ring,
   And rest in Orion's starry belt'" —

"Stop, Puck," said Joy: "if the Culprit Fay could resist such an invitation, surely I ought to. I shall come to you all in good time some day, and come to stay; but do not urge me, for I am afraid if you did I should stay, and I haven't any beautiful heliotypes yet to surprise my friends with when they come here."

"You are right, Joy," said Puck sadly; "remember what a gentle poetess who loved the stars said of one that faded out of the Sky-Garden, and was lost forever to mortal view."

Then all grew confused and giddy to Joy. She could see nothing distinctly; but she could hear several voices calling her by name, and saying, "Where is Joy? Where can that child have gone?" Then she felt her mother's arms about her, and heard her say, "Why, darling, you must have been walking in your sleep. Did you know that you were standing on the verge of the observatory-roof when we found you? Your papa has been up all night watching the meteoric shower. Just before dawn there was such a magnificent display that he called us all up to see it. You were not in your bed; and, when I rushed up to tell your papa, our attention was attracted by a superb falling star; and just as it sunk out of sight we saw you standing where it disappeared, like a little white ghost."

"I suppose I must have slipped off of it," said Joy musingly; and then they all laughed, and her father carried her down to her bed, saying that she was not thoroughly awake. But, as soon as they left her, Joy

stole to her book-case, and, taking down a volume of
Jean Ingelow that Cousin Myrtle had given her as a
parting gift, read the passage that Puck had referred to
just before she left him : —

> " More than content were I, my race being run,
>   Might it be true of me, though none thereon
>   Should muse regretful, ' While she lived, she shone.' "